Dracula: The Musical?

Book, Music & Lyrics by
Rick Abbot

SAMUELFRENCH.COM   SAMUELFRENCH.CO.UK

FOR PRODUCTION ENQUIRIES

UNITED STATES AND CANADA
Info@SamuelFrench.com
1-866-598-8449

UNITED KINGDOM AND EUROPE
Plays@SamuelFrench.co.uk
020-7255-4302

Each title is subject to availability from Samuel French, depending upon country of performance. Please be aware that *DRACULA: THE MUSICAL?* may not be licensed by Samuel French in your territory. Professional and amateur producers should contact the nearest Samuel French office or licensing partner to verify availability.

Please refer to page 70 for further copyright information.

Dracula:
The *Musical*?

CAST OF CHARACTERS

DR. SAM SEWARD . . . . genial proprietor of a madhouse
MINA SEWARD . . . . the doctor's discontented daughter
SOPHIE SEWARD . . . . Mina's mother and Sam's spouse
BUBU PADOOP . . . . a frisky friend of the family
NELLY NORTON . . . . the maid at the madhouse
BORIS RENFIELD . . . . one of Sam's peculiar patients
DR. VAN HELSING . . . . a stalwart exterminator
*COUNT DRACULA . . . . a newcomer to the neighborhood
*JONATHAN HARKER . . . . a mysteriously missing realtor

*[dual role for one actor]

TIME: *The mid-1800s*
PLACE: *The Seward family madhouse, a short gallop from London.*

ACT ONE: An August evening just before dinner
ACT TWO: Shortly before dawn the following day

———*———

**This show is fondly dedicated
to ABBOTT and PETER, for
their years of encouragement,
friendship and staunch support.**

Dracula:
The *Musical*?

MUSICAL NUMBERS

ACT ONE

OVERTURE .... Accompanist
1) VOCATIONAL REFLECTION .... Sam
2) I LOVE THE NIGHT! .... Mina, Bubu
3) WHERE WAS I? .... Boris
4) ALONE! .... Dracula
5) A WONDERFUL PLACE TO WORK .... Nelly
6) HOW OUTRAGEOUS! ... Van, Mina, Bubu, Nelly, Sophie
7) DON'T BE AFRAID! .... Dracula
8) WHERE WAS I? (1st reprise) .... Boris
9) COME INTO MY WORLD .... Dracula, Mina
10) STUPID SUPERSTITION ...... Sam, Sophie, Nelly, Bubu

ACT TWO

ENTR'ACTE .... Accompanist
11) THE LADY IN WHITE .... Sophie, Bubu, Nelly
12) I'D MAKE A HORRID HUSBAND .... Van, Bubu
13) WHERE WAS I? (2nd reprise) .... Boris
14) DON'T BE AFRAID! (reprise) .... Dracula, Nelly
15) YOU HAVEN'T GOT A CHANCE! .... Dracula
16) WHERE WAS I? (final reprise) .... Boris
17) AT LAST! (Finale) .... All Survivors

Dracula:
The *Musical?*

ACT ONE

*Curtain rises on the parlor of the Seward madhouse, on an Au-
gust evening just before 8 p.m. Starting at* D.R., *we see a
desk and chair [see SPECIAL EFFECTS] with a built-in
bookcase just over the rear of the desk; halfway* U. *from
this, we see a pier table holding an old-fashioned telephone
(the earpiece-on-receiver sort), on the wall above which is a
large (at least 2′ wide by 3′ high) mirror [see SPECIAL EF-
FECTS]; immediately above this is a broad platform about
8″ high, which occupies the entire* U. *area (about half the
breadth of the proscenium width); an archway at the ex-
treme right of this platform gives access to the cells of the
madhouse and the family bedrooms; centered* U. *on the platform are wide-open french doors leading to a partly-seen
railed balcony, beyond which is visible only black night sky;
then, in mirror-image relation to the foregoing, moving
down the left wall, we see a pier table containing a tall vase
filled with tall flowers [see SPECIAL EFFECTS], just
below another archway at platform-level which gives access
to the front part of the building (dining room, front hall,
etc.); directly opposite the desk is a tall fireplace [see
SPECIAL EFFECTS], before which is a wingbacked chaise
longue parallel to the angle of the fireplace, its foot toward
the proscenium; at the very* C. *of the stage area below the
platform is a wide sofa, flanked by matching endtables, and
having a broad table holding liquor, soda siphon, ice
bucket, glasses, etc., set flush along the back of the sofa.
General ambience is of sedate good taste and quietly middle-
class elegance suitable to the 19th century. [NOTE: For
simplicity's sake, entrances and exits from the room will be*

designated simply by location, thusly: U.R. = *bedroom/cell archway,* U.L. = *archway to front of building,* U.C. = *upstage french doors,* D.R. = *via trick desk, and DL = via trick fireplace.]*
At curtain-rise, stage is empty and PHONE IS RINGING. After a moment, NELLY NORTON *enters in maid's uniform* U.L., *crosses to phone and answers it.*

NELLY. (*On phone.*) Hello? . . . Who? . . . How do you spell that? . . . No, I'm sorry, there's no one of that name here. You must have the wrong number. (*DOORBELL—actually a deep and sonorous gong—RINGS.*) Oh, there's the doorbell, I've got to go. (*Hangs up, starts for* U.L., *but pauses just short of exit as* MINA SEWARD, *a lovely young woman in an evening gown, enters* U.R. *and speaks to her.*)
MINA. Nelly, who was on the phone?
NELLY. A wrong number, Miss Mina. Why, are you expecting a call?
MINA. Well—no, not exactly. I just thought it might be . . . Jonathan. Or at least some word about him.
NELLY. No such luck, Miss. I'm sorry. (*DOORBELL RINGS again.*) Excuse me, I'd better answer that! (*NELLY starts out, and* MINA *moves down to table where she will pour herself a drink; as she is in the process of doing so,* SAM SEWARD, *a rubicund and jolly man of middle age, in immaculate evening clothes, will enter* U.R., *see her, smile, and start toward her, on:*)
SAM. Ah, there you are, Mina! My, how lovely you look!
MINA. What—? Oh, Father, it's you. My mind was rather—distracted.
SAM. Still mooning about your missing fiance? (*Will start to fix two drinks.*) Well, I wouldn't worry *too* much about it, my dear. Any number of reasons we might not have heard from him—monsoon season—shipping strike—train connections—the possibilities are endless.
MINA. (*Strolling over to gaze into fireplace, carrying her drink, while* SAM *finishes pouring two drinks.*) Oh, I know I'm just being a silly goose, Father. And yet—and yet—there's this nameless dread that keeps nagging at me—! (*SOPHIE SEWARD enters* U.R., *a middle-aged woman in an evening gown, and moves down toward* SAM, *during:*)
SAM. Nonsense! Put it out of your mind! Jonathan can take care of himself. (*Sees* SOPHIE.) Ah, Sophie! Just in time! Here you are, my dear. (*Hands one of two drinks to her.*)

SOPHIE. Thank you, Sam. (*Takes sip of drink, then starts toward* MINA, *as* SAM, *carrying his own drink, strolls* U. *to gaze idly out at night sky; she speaks en route.*) Mina, my dear, you mustn't fret so. After all, Count Dracula is coming to dinner, tonight, and he will most certainly have some word about Jonathan.

MINA. (*Turns from fireplace to face her.*) Oh, Mother, do you really think so?

SOPHIE. Well, darling, he *is* the reason Jonathan went off to Transylvania in the *first* place, to sell him that lovely castle just across the swamp from our little madhouse . . .

SAM. (*Turns with a scowl.*) Sophie, I do wish you wouldn't use that term. I much prefer "sanatarium."

SOPHIE. Call it what you like, Sam, this is a *house*, and most of the people in it have gone *mad*, so why you quibble about what *name* to give it — !

SAM. (*Will move* D. *to point between chaise and sofa; at same time,* SOPHIE *will stroll over and sit at left end of sofa, while* MINA *will take a seat on lower right edge of chaise.*) Psychology, Sophie, psychology! After all, "madhouse" sounds like a place where the screwballs are simply *locked up*, whereas "sanatarium" suggests an insitution where people come to be *cured*!

SOPHIE. But you haven't cured *one* of them!

SAM. (*Now at mid-sofa-chaise point, scowls.*) I am *doing* the best I *can*!

MINA. Oh, but Father, how I wish you were in a more pleasant line of work!

SAM. (*Shrugs.*) A calling is a calling. When the summons sounds, a man must follow! (*MUSIC intros, and he sings.*)
SOME MEN GO SAILING OUT TO SEA,
SOME LEAD A REVOLUTION.
LIVES HAVE DESIGN,
AND I'VE FOUND MINE:
I BELONG IN AN INSTITUTION!
SOME THRILL AT CHOPPING DOWN A TREE,
SOME TAKE UP ELOCUTION.
EACH MAN MUST FIND
WHERE HE'S ASSIGNED.
I BELONG IN AN INSTITUTION!
MANY NEVER KNOW WHERE THEY OUGHT TO GO;
THEY LIVE OUT THEIR LIVES AS SAD MEN!
BUT LUCKY OLD ME! IT'S EASY TO BE

THE GLADDEST OF GLAD MEN
HERE WITH MY MADMEN!
SOME BEG A FEE FOR CHARITY,
SOME MAKE THE CONTRIBUTION.
BUT, WHY DENY
MY CALLING? I
BELONG IN AN INSTITUTION!
I RELISH THE
INSANE AUTHORITY
EV'RYBODY KNOWS I'M CRACKED . . .

> (*Women look at him, startled, but relax*
> *again as he completes the phrase.*)

UP TO BE!

> (*Drains his drink contentedly.*)

SOPHIE. Well, I suppose this lifestyle beats living in the poorhouse. (*Stands.*) But not by much. (*Drains her own drink, moves up right of sofa as* SAM *moves up left of it, and both set their empty glasses on table, during:*)

MINA. I think the worst part of it is the sleeping arrangements. (*Stands.*) I wish our bedrooms weren't right there beside the cell block.

SAM. There's really nothing to *fear*, Mina. All the bedroom doors have stout iron bolts.

MINA. Yes. On the *out*side!

SOPHIE. A mere architect's oversight. (*Moves down right of sofa, strolls to hearth to warm her hands near the fire, as* MINA *moves up toward flowers on pier table.*) I *do* wish he'd installed central heating, though. Lately the nights are unusually chilly for August.

SAM. (*Still U. of table, thoughtfully.*) They are, aren't they! Ever since Count Dracula moved in across the way. Coincidence, of course.

MINA. (*Pauses in her idle inspection of flowers to look at him.*) I'm—I'm not so sure. Ever since he moved in there, I feel this dreadful sense of cold—of darkness—of doom—

SOPHIE. You're talking nonsense. Why, whatever can the count have to do with the weather?

MINA. It's not the outside air so much . . . it's here— (*A hand to her breast.*) Deep inside me. The strangest sensation . . . as of some hidden danger . . .

SAM. But my dear, you've not even met the man!

MINA. Nor am I sure I want to.

SOPHIE. Mina, what a thing to say! Mind your manners. After all, the man is royalty!

MINA. History is filled with accounts of wicked kings — why not counts? (*Looks right, as* BUBU PADOOP, *a pretty young lady in a frilly evening gown, enters* U.R..) Bubu! Where in the world have you been? It's nearly dinnertime.

BUBU. (*Crossing to her.*) Changing gowns. I must have tried on half a dozen before I found one that seemed suitable.

SAM. Suitable for what?

BUBU. Why, meeting this Count Dracula, of course! I hear he's ever so handsome. I want to make a good first impression.

SOPHIE. Yes, my dear, of course, but — isn't that gown rather — daring?

SAM. Nonsense. Delightful dress. Bubu is a lovely young lady, no matter what she wears, of course — but there's much to be said for proper packaging! (SOPHIE *will move to* SAM, *and the two of them will then move toward* U.C., *as* MINA *and* BUBU *move to table,* MINA *to discard her empty glass,* BUBU *to pour a drink of her own, during:*)

BUBU. It *is* rather striking, isn't it! It's one of my costumes from the last show I was in.

SAM. Do you know — *I've* often thought about writing for the theatre.

SOPHIE. Why, Sam! You've never mentioned it to *me*.

SAM. Oh, just a whim, of course. (*He and* SOPHIE *are now framed in* U.C. *doorway, looking back toward twosome at table.*) Haven't worked out much more than the opening moments of the show, really.

MINA. Why, how exciting! Tell us, Father, do!

SAM. (*Rather embarrassed, but subtly proud.*) Oh, well — you know how in simply dreadful plays, the first act opens with the maid answering the telephone, and she manages to give out all sorts of vital information to the audience — ? Well, I thought it would be a real hoot if one began a play like that, and then instead of giving information, it would turn out that the call was simply a wrong number!

SOPHIE. What a cute idea!

BUBU. Yes, but there's only one thing wrong with it: The telephone hasn't been invented yet! (*As* OTHERS *react, a number of things happen: The* STAGE MANAGER *[you may use your own, here] enters* U.L., *hastens over to telephone [which is not corded into a phone outlet, of course], picks it up, and starts back toward* U.L. *with it, at the same time* NELLY *hastens in from* U.R. *with a low bowl of flowers [so they won't block our view of the mirror], places them in the spot where the phone had been, and exits* U.R. *fast, disappearing just at the moment the* STAGE MANAGER *is at* U.L. *archway, at which time he pauses, looks out at audience with an embarrassed grin, shrugs, and then exits; during all the foregoing, the foursome onstage remain where they are, expressionless, and then they continue the play as if nothing had happened.*)

SAM. Shall we stroll on the balcony, my dear? The moon will soon be rising behind Dracula's castle. It's quite an awesome sight.

SOPHIE. Oh, yes, let's do! (*They exit* U.C., *moving from view toward right.*)

BUBU. Brrr! How can they stand it! A black sky, a full moon, and all those spiky battlements silhouetted against the blackness. Me for high noon, any time of day! (*Takes fortifying sip of her drink.*)

MINA. Oh, but Bubu, there's something so marvelous about the hours of darkness! A sort of peaceful shroud settling over the world . . .

BUBU. Kiddo, you've been living in a nuthouse too long!

MINA. But it's so quiet, so peaceful, so still—!

BUBU. You could use that same description for a corpse!

MINA. I don't care! Whatever the reason, it stirs some sort of softly soothing sensation deep inside me! (*MUSIC intros and she sings.*)

I LOVE THE NIGHT!
I LOVE ITS MYSTERY!
THE MOON IN FLIGHT INVITES MY HEART!
THE NIGHT BRINGS PEACE
TO SOOTHE AWAY ALL CARE AND SORROW!
WHO CAN BEAR TOMORROW
WHEN DARKNESS MUST DEPART?
STAY ON, SWEET NIGHT!
STAY ON AND COMFORT ME!
CAN YOU NOT BAR TOMORROW'S START?
OH, WISHING STAR
SO FAR,
PLEASE GRANT MY HEART'S DELIGHT:
HOLD BACK THE DAWN
AND LET ME HAVE THE NIGHT!

(MINA *will repeat song second time, but during her reprise,*
   BUBU *will interpolate a sprightly lyric of her own, in counter-*
   point, and by song's end, MINA *is singing as briskly and*
   liltingly with BUBU *as she had been singing yearningly and*
   poignantly during her solo; this all occurs during:)
BUBU. (*Singing contrapuntally.*)
MAYBE THE NIGHT'S ALL RIGHT FOR PITCHING WOO,
BUT THERE ARE THINGS YOU NEED THE SUN TO DO:
GROWING A ROSE OR HANGING THE CLOTHES
TO DRY!
AND, IF I BOUGHT YOUR PLAN,
HOW COULD I GET A TAN
OR POUR MYSELF A GLASS OF WHISKEY?
DRINKING IN THE DARK'S RISKY!
TAKING A TRIP YOU WANT TO SEE EACH SIGHT!
WHY VIEW THE TAJ MAHAL BY CANDLELIGHT?
COLD MIDNIGHT AIR FOR DRYING MY HAIR I SHUN!
NIGHT TIME MIGHT BE FINE IF YOU
HAVE A RENDEZVOUS WITH A CHARMER,
BUT FOR FIXING ONE'S FACE,
I'D VOTE FOR A PLACE IN THE SUN FOR ANYONE!
   MINA. (*Laughing at song's end.*) Oh, Bubu, I'm *so* glad you've
come to stay with us awhile! I *need* cheering up. I've been ever so
maudlin since Jonathan vanished!
   BUBU. I know what you mean! A woman's not really complete
unless she has a *man* around! (BORIS RENFIELD, *a wild-haired,*
sly-eyed inmate, in a sort of pajama-type uniform, and
barefooted, springs into view via U.R. *archway, landing in a*
half-crouch, smiling crazily, and just remains there, looking at
them, for:) Present company excepted!
   MINA. Oh, that's only Boris Renfield, one of the maniacs.
   BUBU. Renfield? Isn't he the one who eats mosquitos, flies and
spiders?!
   MINA. Yes; but think what we save on swatters! (*Moves*
toward him.) Good evening, Boris!
   BUBU. (*Rushes to her, eagerly shakes her hand.*) Good evening, Miss Mina! So nice of your father to ask me to join you for
dinner!
   BUBU. Dinner? You're joining us for dinner? In heaven's
name, *why*?!
   MINA. (*Leading* BORIS—*who walks with a monkeyish*
lope—*down toward* BUBU.) It was Mother's idea. After all, there

would have only been the five of us for dinner, other-wise—Mother thinks there should be equal numbers of men and women at table, even if one of them *is* a little loony.

BUBU. You know, maybe *she's* been living in a nuthouse too long, herself!

MINA. (*Will lead* BORIS *down right of sofa, and* BUBU—*leaving her emptied glass on table—will come down left of it and join them seated on sofa,* BORIS *in* C., *during:*) He's really quite harmless. Just a bit disgusting, is all. And he has fewer aberrations than many of the inmates.

BUBU. You mean there's something besides his unusual appetite?

MINA. Well—yes. (*Lowers her voice and confides to* BUBU—*though she has to lean directly across* BORIS *to do so.*) He has a rather unusual psychological penchant that my father calls "contagious enthusiasm."

BUBU. (*Half-rises.*) You mean it's catching?!

MINA. Only psychologically.

BUBU. (*Sits back down, but warily.*) Explain that.

MINA. Well, you see, Boris's mother was a gypsy. And, gypsies being what they are, he traveled quite a bit, all his life. So we have to be very careful what we say to him, because any mention of any place he's ever been provokes a sort of—um—*reaction* in him.

BUBU. (*Very wary, now.*) What—what *sort* of reaction?

MINA. He—does travelogues.

BUBU. (*Reacts with blinking incredulity.*) Travelogues? *That* doesn't sound so bad. I mean, why *shouldn't* he? If you've been to a place, and feel like talking about it—

MINA. It's not that. It's—the *way* he gives them. That's where the "contagious" part comes in. He gets listeners so excited that—

BUBU. That *what*?

MINA. (*Abruptly draws back, becomes incommunicative.*) I—I hope you never find out.

BUBU. Oh, but Mina—!

MINA. (*Primly.*) No. No, I've said far too much already. It's not really polite to discuss our patients' problems with outsiders.

BUBU. Aw, come on! I'm practically one of the family! Tell me! If we mention a place he's been, and he gives his little travelogue—what happens next?

MINA. Let's drop the topic. I'd really rather not say. (SAM *and* SOPHIE *re-enter* U.C., *move toward group.*)

SAM. Ah, Renfield! Glad you could make it, old chap!

BORIS. It's not as if I had anyplace *else* to go.

SOPHIE. Oh, but, Minster Renfield—you didn't dress for dinner!

BORIS. This is all the clothes I've got. They took all my other things away, when they brought me here.

BUBU. (*Kindheartedly.*) Don't you fret, Boris. You're not really so badly dressed—it's just that the rest of us are in such *fancy* togs. In fact— (*Starts to get up.*) I'll change into something simpler, if you like!

SOPHIE. (*Who is at left end of sofa, standing, as is* SAM *similarly at right end.*) No need, dear. I simply forgot about Mister Renfield's lack of clothing for the moment. I don't mind the way he looks, really.

BUBU. (*Sits down again.*) Well—all right. But it would have been such a nice excuse for getting out of this evening gown and wearing something simpler, like perhaps, my new jersey—

BORIS. (*Springs wildly to his feet, wild-eyed.*) *New Jersey!* (*From now on, in the play, whenever one of these "trigger" words are echoed by* BORIS, *all* OTHERS *in the room will react with trapped horror of what is to follow; this one time, of course, only the three* SEWARDS *do so;* BUBU *is bewildered, but not apprehensive, this time only; in later reprises of this maniacal moment, she will react exactly as do the others, frozen in apprehension as he sings.*)

A STATE THAT I THOUGHT WAS SO VERY NICE!

IF YOU'LL TAKE MY ADVICE,

YOU'LL TURN YOUR FACES TO

THE PLACES YOU CAN SEE . . .

IN GOOD OLD NEW JER-SEY . . . !

(*Now music takes on gypsy quality, a slow* czardas *tempo, beginning rhythmically and meticulously, but increasing in tempo and volume until it finishes in an absolute frenzy of lyrical speed.*)

THERE'S PATERSON, AND ITTY-BITTY

TETERBORO, JERSEY CITY,

RUTHERFORD WHERE ROADS ARE ROCKY,

LITTLE FERRY AND MOONACHIE,

PALISADES PARK WITH ITS RIDES,

AND PRINCETON, CRANFORD,

PEAPACK, HACKENSACK,

AND GOOD OLD NEWARK, BESIDES!

(*And now we learn the reason for* MINA'S *reticence, as* MELODY *repeats, while* BORIS *goes into fast and frantic gypsy dance — and* OTHERS *instantly* start the same dance when he does — *everybody whirling, clapping hands, leaping about the room, and shouting "Hey!" every eight beats, until completion of melody, at which moment each person is back in spot where he or she was at moment dancing began, and each instantly* becomes serenely calm, as if nothing had happened.)

BUBU. (*After a silence, turns her head to look past* BORIS *toward* MINA, *and observes quietly.*) I see what you mean. (NELLY *appears at* U.L. *archway, takes stance, and:*)

NELLY. Count Dracula! (*She steps back [upstage], and* COUNT DRACULA *enters; he is tall, dark, ferally handsome, in evening dress, and wearing a long black red-lined cloak; he stands there smiling at group,* ALL *of whom have shifted position to look his way.*)

DRACULA. Good evening! (*He makes a gesture of greeting with his left hand and arm, and as he does so, flowers on left pier table instantly wilt, droop and dangle limply over lip of vase [see SPECIAL EFFECTS]; if you can find a sound-effect to accompany this metamorphosis [such as a low whistling sound that* glissandos *down an octave to match the motion of the flowers], so much the better.*) I hope my tardiness has not delayed your dinner?

SAM. Not at all, not at all! (*Starts up toward him.*) Nelly, why haven't you taken the count's cloak?

NELLY. He wouldn't *let* me, sir. I tried, honestly I did!

DRACULA. The maid speaks the truth. It is an idiosyncrasy of mine. I hope you do not object?

SAM. Naturally not. Whatever makes you comfortable is fine by me! But come, Count Dracula, and meet the rest of our dinner party!

NELLY. (*As* SAM *escorts* DRACULA *down right of sofa.*) Will there be anything else, Doctor Seward?

SAM. Not just now, Nelly. Thank you.

NELLY. Very good, sir. (*Exits* U.L..)

SAM. (*As he and* DRACULA *draws abreast of group.*) Count Dracula — I should like you to meet my wife, Sophie —

SOPHIE. (*With a slight curtsey, since she is standing.*) My dear Count.

DRACULA. Charmed.

SAM. A friend of the family, Miss Bubu Padoop —

BUBU. (*With a nod, since she is seated.*) Count Dracula.

DRACULA. Delighted.

SAM. One of my patients, Mister Boris Renfield—

BORIS. (*Slides deftly off sofa, twisting to his right, to land on his knees facing* DRACULA, *and bowing like a Mohammedan praying toward Mecca.*) Master!

DRACULA. Flattered.

SAM. And my dear daughter Mina.

MINA. (*Who has been staring at him in something of a daze.*) Have—have we met, before—?

DRACULA. I think not, Mina. I would surely not forget such a lovely face. (*Bows, takes her right hand, kisses it, straightens.*)

MINA. (*Rises, faces him, still in that dazed fashion.*) Can I—offer you something to drink—?

DRACULA. (*Leans toward her hungrily, then restrains himself.*) Later, perhaps.

SAM. (*Briskly, sensing nothing amiss.*) Well, now that *that's* out of the way, shall we go down to dinner?

SOPHIE. Oh, yes, let's. I'm simply famished! (*She will move up left of sofa and cross above it to* SAM, *near its upper right end, while* BORIS—*getting to his feet quickly—takes* BUBU's *arm and leads her up left of sofa toward* U.L. *exit,* SAM *and* SOPHIE *moving after them, but a few paces to their rear, during:*)

SOPHIE. Oh, by the way, Mina dear, don't forget to ask Count Dracula for information about Jonathan!

MINA. (*Still standing staring blankly into* DRACULA's *face.*) . . . Jonathan *who?* (*Departing foursome stop in unison, look her way.*)

BUBU. Harker. Jonathan Harker. Your fiance. You can't have forgotten?

MINA. (*Snapping slightly out of it.*) What—? Oh. No, of course I haven't. I'll ask him right now—and then we'll come join you all in the dining room.

SAM. (*As foursome starts out again.*) Very well, very well. Don't be too long about it, now . . .

SOPHIE. (*Glancing toward vase as they exit.*) Oh, dear, *look* at those flowers! I must send Nelly back with some fresh ones. What *will* the dear count think of us! (*Foursome are gone.*)

MINA. (*The mesmerizing moment is past, and now she is just a bit uneasy.*) I—um—I *do* hope you *can* be of some help, Count Dracula—?

DRACULA. (*Leans insinuatingly closer to her.*) Tell me what you would like me to do . . .

MINA. (*To avoid those eyes, moves suddenly downstage of*

and past him, hurrying to desk, which she will lean on with both hands, suddenly breathless; all this during.) It's just — information. That's all. About my missing fiance. He — Jonathan Harker, that is — went to Hungary more than two months ago, to find your castle there — in the Carpathian Mountains, I believe — (*She is now at desk, trying to breathe quietly.*)

DRACULA. (*Moving softly after her.*) Yes, that is correct, my dear. Though my actual residence is in Transylvania — a part of Hungary — but I am Hungarian, nonetheless.

MINA. (*Turns to speak; reacts to find him unexpectedly near.*) Oh! . . . I mean — Oh, I see. But — he did *get* there, didn't he? — No, wait — I'm being foolish — if he hadn't gotten there, then you wouldn't be here, since he could not have leased the property to you, and — and — (*Realizes.*) I'm babbling. Why am I babbling? I've never babbled in my life!

DRACULA. Perhaps you are — afraid?

MINA. (*Unconvincingly.*) Of you? Nonsense. Never. I mean — why *should* I be? Just because you're so tall — and so strong — and have the sharpest-looking teeth — and we're all alone here in this room . . .! (*Her fear has become more apparent with each addition to her list; now she falls silent, staring at him.*)

DRACULA. But at least there are *two* of us. That is not so terrible a loneliness as it might be. When one is *truly* alone — cut off from *everybody* else — it is the loneliness of the grave!

MINA. (*Leaning backward, the heels of her hands on the desk.*) What are you saying? What do you want? What is it you're trying to make me say — make me do — ?!

DRACULA. (*Abruptly straightens, takes a short backstep.*) Nothing. Truly nothing. I would not *force* you to do anything. It must not be that way. When you come to me — it must be of your own accord! (*MUSIC intros and he sings.*)
YOUR WILLINGNESS I CRAVE!
YOU NEEDN'T BE A SLAVE!
CAN YOU NOT UNDERSTAND
THE THINGS I'VE PLANNED?
IF I CAN'T WAKEN YOUR TRUST,
EV'RYTHING TURNS TO DUST!
(*Takes her hands; she flinches slightly, but as he continues singing, she slowly moves closer and closer to him, her gaze locked on his face with increasing longing and irresistable desire.*)
SO COME AWAY TO JOYS YOU'VE NEVER KNOWN!

SHARE MY LOVE IN UNEXPLORED DELIGHT
BEFORE THE NIGHT HAS FLOWN . . .
WHAT JOY IS THERE ALONE . . .
ALONE . . . ALONE . . .?!

(*At song's end, he pulls her gently to him; her eyes close; her head leans backward; he lowers his mouth toward the left side of her throat . . . and* NELLY *comes bustling in* U.L., *with a tall vase of fresh flowers.*)

NELLY. (*Brightly, as she moves down to pier table, where she will swap limp flowers for the fresh ones, vase and all.*) Hey, you guys, soup's on! (*Startled,* DRACULA *springs back, and* MINA *comes out of her trance, reacts to his nearness, and edges* U. *toward mirror, keeping an eye on him.*) You're missing your dinner!

DRACULA. (*Annoyed, chagrined.*) I most certainly am!

MINA. (*Hastily, turns to mirror, where we see her reflection as she perfunctorily pats at a few stray hairs.*) Yes, we really must go down—Father will be furious if we're late! (*He moves* U. *toward her, but she moves swiftly toward* U.L., *pausing just short of exit.*) Coming, Count—?

DRACULA. (*Giving it up.*) Certainly, my dear. Right away. (*She turns and exits, but he reaches mirror—where we see* no *reflection at all [see SPECIAL EFFECTS]—and* NELLY—*at opposite pier table, sees the same thing and gapes in surprise as he adjusts his bowtie as if seeing himself in the blank glass, then moves* U.L. *on:*) We can always become better acquainted—*after* dinner—! (*Exits.*)

NELLY. (*As soon as he's gone, looks out front, uneasily.*) Yipe. (*Sets wilted flowers in their vase near foot of pier table.*) I must be imagining things. (*Crosses apprehensively toward mirror, sees her reflection therein, and sighs and sags in great relief.*) Wow, *that's* a relief! Must've been a trick of the lights, or something. Nothing abnormal going on at all. (*Takes two steps back toward vase, stops.*) Except that I'm *talking* to myself! (*Clasps her hands, wringing them slightly as she moves* D., *facing us, on:*) I've got to calm down. I'm letting this job *get* to me. (*With slightly restored aplomb, moves farther* D., *right of sofa; during her upcoming song, she will move here and there in room—to desk, to fireplace, etc.—but end up beside limpflowered vase at pier table.*) So it's a nuthouse—so what! Lots of crazies in the *outside* world, *right*? At least in here you can recognize them by their uniforms! . . . Nelly Norton, you are

still talking to yourself! . . . And why? What is there to be afraid of? (*MUSIC intros, and she sings.*)
THOUGH THE NIGHTS HERE ARE AS BLACK
AS INK,
AND MY SANITY IS ON THE BRINK
AS EACH PSYCHOPATHIC KINK
STARTS DRIVING ME TO DRINK—
STILL, ALL IN ALL, I LIKE TO THINK . . .
IT'S SUCH A
WONDERFUL PLACE TO WORK!
DOCTOR SEWARD'S BUS'NESS MAY DEPOSIT
FIENDS IN EV'RY CLOSET,
BUT THOUGH SOME DANGERS LURK,
AND MY HEART IS BEATING LIKE A HAMMER
IN THIS PSYCHO SLAMMER,
I'M RATHER GLAD,
'CAUSE THE PAY ISN'T BAD.
IF THE PATIENTS ARE MAD
AS A HATTER,
IT DOESN'T MATTER,
FOR, OUT IN THE MIST AND MURK
JUST BEYOND OUR GATE,
WHO KNOWS WHAT DANGERS
WAIT WITH HANDSOME STRANGERS?
BUT HERE THE NUTS, YOU SEE,
ARE UNDER LOCK AND KEY!
SO WORKING HERE IS QUITE ALL RIGHT WITH ME!
THERE'S NO GUESSWORK HERE!
OUTSIDE, THE CRAZY FOLKS ARE WALKING FREE!
IT'S MUCH LESS WORK HERE
TO KNOW FOR SURE WHOSE BRAIN IS
UPSIDE-DOWN . . .!
(*Is at vase of wilted flowers now; picks it up and pauses just short of* U.L. *exit to finish, out front.*)
PLUS IT'S THE ONLY JOB IN TOWN!
(*Exits; a moment later, we hear a CRASH, as of a dropped vase, and she backs into room again, empty-handed, looking startled, as* DOCTOR VAN HELSING, *in overcoat and slouch hat, enters* U.L.)
Who are you? What do you want? Don't touch me or I'll scream the house down!
    VAN. Ssh! I mean no harm. I am Doctor Van Helsing! I must see Doctor Seward at once on a matter of the gravest urgency!

NELLY. Do you have an appointment?

VAN. (*Icily.*) I am *not* a *mental* patient! I have come to warn Seward that an undying monster is stalking this household!

NELLY. (*Very dubious.*) You sure *sound* like a mental patient!

VAN. (*Maintaining his self-control.*) Young lady, I *know* it *sounds* that way, but I assure you it is nevertheless the truth. *Will* you get the doctor, or shall *I* seek him out?

NELLY. (*Relenting.*) Oh, what the hell, I'll get him. Um . . . who did you say is calling — ?

VAN. (*Relieved.*) Doctor Van Helsing. And be sure to tell him the dire urgency of my visit. There are certain things that are so horrible they should be destroyed on sight!

NELLY. (*Doing her duty.*) Your hat and coat?

VAN. (*Misunderstanding.*) Of *course* not!

NELLY. (*Misunderstanding.*) Then whose *are* they?

VAN. (*Finally catching her drift.*) Oh! You mean — you want to *take* them! (*Starts removing them.*) Excuse my confusion — I'm quite overwrought, I fear.

NELLY. Are you *sure* you're not a patient?

VAN. (*Hands her the garments, stands revealed as a man of* SEWARD'S *age, but a good deal trimmer, almost gaunt.*) Trust me!

NELLY. (*Takes garments.*) That's what they *all* say! (*She turns to exit* U.L., *but stops as* MINA, BUBU *and* SOPHIE *re-enter, apprehensive and curious.*)

SOPHIE. Nelly!

BUBU. What was that awful crash?

MINA. And who is this unexpected stranger?

BUBU. (*Sizing him up.*) This unexpected *handsome* stranger!

NELLY. The crash was the vase I dropped when he popped up in the hall and scared the pants off me. As to his name —

VAN. My name is Van Helsing. *Doctor* Van Helsing. (NELLY, *since he picked up the conversational ball, exits* U.L. *with his hat and coat, during:*)

BUBU. Ooh, a *doctor*! (*Moves closer to him.*) Are you married?

VAN. (*Uncertainly.*) Why . . . no.

BUBU. (*Links arms with him.*) Marvelous! May I call you "Van"?

VAN. But — my first name is "Hezekiah".

BUBU. All the more reason.

SOPHIE. My dear sir, I hope you haven't come to dine with us, because I deplore having an odd number at the table.

MINA. Then why did you invite Count Dracula?

BUBU. Yeah, he's one of the *oddest* numbers I've *ever* met!

VAN. (*Pulls free of* BUBU, *takes a backstep.*) Dracula! Here! Then I may *already* be too late!

BUBU. Oh, no, there's *plenty* of dinner to go around.

NELLY. (*Re-enters* U.L..) Doctor Van Helsing, Doctor Seward says he will join you here in just a few moments.

VAN. Ah, then you conveyed to him the urgency of my quest?

NELLY. Well, I said you were ready to freak out, if that's what you mean.

VAN. (*Rubbing his palms together, moves* D., *the* OTHERS *following him curiously, on.*) Good, good. And what of his bizarre guest?

NELLY. Count Dracula? It's the oddest thing, but—when I mentioned your name—he got a funny look on his face and said he'd take a stroll in the garden for awhile.

MINA. Doctor, is *that* what brought you here? Count Dracula? Then there *is* something strange about him! I sensed it from the start! (*By now,* ALL *are gathered* D. *of sofa.*)

VAN. You are fortunate, young lady. Most persons do not realize the danger until it is too late!

SOPHIE. Danger? What danger?

VAN. You may all be in jeopardy from the intended depredations of an unspeakably ravenous creature of the undead!

BUBU. How's that again?

VAN. (*Takes stance right of sofa, where—positioned from right to left—*MINA, BUBU *and* SOPHIE *now seat themselves,* NELLY *remaining standing left of sofa; he speaks solemnly.*) Have you all heard the legend of the—vampire? A creature who prowls the night, not dead yet not alive, who must draw his sustenance from the veins of the living?

SOPHIE. (*With practicality.*) Well, we've heard it *now*!

MINA. But such things are mere peasant superstitions!

BUBU. Surely *you* don't believe such a thing, Doctor?

NELLY. And even if you *do*, what's it got to do with *us*?

VAN. I believe Count Dracula may be such a creature!

SOPHIE. *Now* he tells us!

MINA. But Doctor—how can one be *sure*?

VAN. There are many signs. His nearness can wilt flowers—

SOPHIE. Oh!

VAN. He casts no reflection in a mirror—

NELLY. Oh!

VAN. One glance from his burning eyes can bind you to his will—

MINA. Oh!

VAN. And he must return to his coffin before sunrise, or die! (SOPHIE, NELLY and MINA — *since each has reacted to a sudden memory of each item* VAN *described — now all look toward* BUBU *for her own commentary, but:*)

BUBU. I pass.

VAN. There is no time to tell you all the details right now. You must take my warning on faith.

SOPHIE. Well — actually — I *have* heard a *little* bit about vampires . . .

MINA. Me, too. But I always thought it was a myth.

BUBU. A flight of fancy.

NELLY. A crock of baloney.

VAN. Ah, would that it were the case! But the legend is quite true!

WOMEN. Oh, *tell* us about it!

VAN. I thought you'd never ask! (*NOTE: The key to the following song number is that, although* VAN *is trying to describe what he deems as terrifying, the* WOMEN *are obviously enthralled by what they hear, and despite their verbal protestations of shock and outrage, they are smiling dreamily at each new comment — but trying not to show their delight to* VAN; *this all begins as he starts to sing.*)

IMAGINE THE TERROR YOU'D FEEL
ENTRAPPED BY TWO ARMS THAT WERE STRONGER
THAN STEEL! TOO FRIGHTENED TO FIGHT
HIS MALIGNANTLY TIGHTENING CLUTCH!

WOMEN. (*Feigning dread for his benefit.*)
OH, DEAR! WE TREMBLE WITH FEAR!

VAN.
DON'T LET HIM GET UNDER YOUR SKIN!
HE CAN'T ENTER WHERE NO ONE BIDS HIM COME IN!
SO THOUGH HE'S INSIDIOUS,
DON'T DREAD HIS HIDEOUS TOUCH!
TELL HIM, "GO AWAY!
DRY UP AND BLOW AWAY!"

WOMEN.
ALL THIS BEHAVIORAL LORE
ON SUCH CREATURES OF GRAVEYARD AND GORE
SIMPLY SETS OUR HEARTS SEETHING
TILL BREATHING GROWS SHORT!

VAN. (*Takes* MINA's *hand.*)
HEARTS WON'T PALPITATE, DEAR, WHEN

TOLD THE FULL REPORT ON HIM!
    MINA.
GIVE US ALL THE DATA, THEN!
    MINA AND OTHER WOMEN.
WHAT'S THE LONG-AND-SHORT ON HIM—?
    VAN. (*Releases* MINA's *hand.*)
EACH NIGHT THE SETTING SUN CAN
RELEASE THIS HIT-AND-RUN MAN
WHO'LL DRAG YOU OFF WHERE NONE CAN
HEAR YOU SCREAMING!
    WOMEN. (TRIO *on sofa stand, forming a foursome with* NELLY,
and all four clasp hands to bosoms rapturously, on:)
HOW OUTRAGEOUS!
    VAN. (*Strolls like lecturing professor, deskward, the* WOMEN
trailing him, moving with choreographed unison, in a balletic
pas de quatre.)
ONE TOUCH OF HIS EMBRACE WILL
ENSLAVE YOU TO HIS BASE WILL,
AND FROM THEN ON HIS FACE WILL
HAUNT YOUR DREAMING!
(*Turns abruptly, sees four smiling faces, starts to react, but*
    WOMEN *instantly face out front, and force facial expressions*
    to convince him they're appalled, on:)
    WOMEN.
HOW OUTRAGEOUS!
    MINA/BUBU.
WE'VE HEARD HE SLEEPS IN A BOX
UNTIL THE MOON COMES UP!
    SOPHIE/NELLY.
THEN WHEN THE LID HE UNLOCKS,
YOUR NUMBER SOON COMES UP!
    VAN. (*Moves to spot between the two foregoing twosomes,*
singing out front as WOMEN *slowly grow ecstatic.*)
AS THE SETTING SUN
SLOWLY DIPS FROM VIEW,
FROM HIS COFFIN HE COMES CRAWLING!
THEN, ONCE HE'S BEGUN,
WITH HIS LIPS ON YOU,
YOU ARE HIS!
    WOMEN.
OH, HOW ENTHRALLING!
        (*Then they react to his shocked look, and emend:*)

THAT IS, WE MEAN, "APPALLING!"

Van. (*Only half-convinced of their sincerity, continues.*)
IF YOU'RE THE ONE HE'S SEEKING,
IT'S FAR TOO LATE FOR SHRIEKING
THE MOMENT HE COMES SNEAKING
NEAR!

Women. (*Surround him soothingly.*)
WELL, HAVE NO FEAR, MY DEAR!
THAT HUNGARIAN HUNK OF CARRION'S
SPELL WON'T TARRY ON WE!
AND IF HE COMES NEAR US,
WE'LL RAISE A FUSS!

Van. (*Relieved.*)
YOU PROMISE ME?

Women. (*Out front, with extra meaning.*)
WE VOW WE'LL CARRY ON . . .
OUTRAGEOUSLY!

(Van *starts to smile, convinced, but then the extra sense of their words gets through to him, and he is about to voice his suspicions when* Sam *and* Boris *enter* U.L. *and interrupt him with:*)

Sam. Van Helsing! (*Starts down toward him, as* Women *all move in a group to fireplace, where they stand chatting [unheard] most enthusiastically and delightedly, during:*) What is this dire news you bring to me?

Van. (*As* Sam *and* Boris *reach him.*) I have reason to suspect that your guest—your new neighbor just across the swamp—Count Dracula—may be a vampire!

Sam. Nonsense! What you suggest is impossible!

Van. But my dear fellow, if you knew the facts—

Sam. I may know more than you think, Van Helsing! And vampire lore itself shows just how wrong you are.

Van. In what way?

Sam. Well, if the legends are true—which I sincerely doubt—one of the basic rules is that a vampire cannot enter into a house unless someone *invites* him in!

Van. But—you invited him to *dinner*, did you not?

Sam. Yes, but you see—this was not his *first* visit to my home. The first time I saw him, he was awaiting me in the parlor downstairs, the sort of anteroom where I meet the families of my patients on occasion. I certainly hadn't invited him in *then*!

Van. (*Disappointed.*) Well—I must admit—you have a telling

point there. He certainly cannot be a vampire if he entered without being invited.

SAM. (*Jovially.*) And when you get right down to it — only a *lunatic* would ask such a creature to come in! (BORIS *reacts, looks ceilingward and starts to whistle as nonchalantly as possible; hearing him,* SAM *does not catch the significance, but simply says:*) Oh, but I'm forgetting my manners! Doctor Van Helsing, I'd like you to meet Boris Renfield, one of my patients.

VAN. (*To* BORIS.) How do you do! (*To* SAM.) What is Mister Renfield's complaint?

SAM. He says his mattress is too hard.

VAN. I mean the nature of his dementia!

SAM. Quite a peculiar one. He dines on bugs.

VAN. But so do the natives of New Guinea. So he could well be as sane as you or I.

BORIS. That's not saying much.

SAM. Ah, but his *other* complaint is *certainly* certifiable! Have you ever heard of "Contagious Enthusiasm Relative to Gypsy Ancestry Manifesting Itself in a Tendency to Guided Tours"?!

VAN. (*Shrugs.*) Of course. Who hasn't! Though I've never *encountered* a case of it.

SAM. (*Claps fond hand on* BORIS's *shoulder.*) Well, you're looking at one!

VAN. Fascinating, fascinating!

BORIS. *Can't* we discuss my dementia over *dinner*—?!

SAM. Splendid idea! (*To* VAN.) You'll join us, of course—?

SOPHIE. (*Catching this last bit, moves toward them.*) Oh, but Sam—that will make an odd number at the table!

NELLY. (*Following* SOPHIE.) No it won't. Count Dracula has gone out.

BUBU. (*Following* NELLY.) But he might come back!

MINA. (*Remaining at fireside.*) Well, don't worry about it. I'm not really very hungry, tonight, anyhow. (*Will recline on chaise during:*) I believe I'll just sit here by the fireside and worry about my missing Jonathan some more. (OTHERS *will move up toward* U.L. — SAM *with* SOPHIE, BUBU *with* VAN, *and* NELLY *and* BORIS *trailing after them—during:*)

SOPHIE. Oh, that reminds me, dear—did Count Dracula know anything of Jonathan's whereabouts?

MINA. I'm not sure—I started to ask him but—somehow—we got off the subject before I ascertained his answer.

SAM. Ah well, time enough to ask him later on, when he returns! (*Exits with* SOPHIE.)

BUBU. You sure you won't join us, Mina—?

MINA. No. Really. You go on and have a nice dinner, Bubu.

VAN. Your name is "Bubu?! Isn't that a little odd?

BUBU. It beats "Hezekiah"! (*Exits with* VAN.)

NELLY. You sure you'll be all right, Miss Mina?

MINA. (*Settling back more comfortably into wingback of chaise.*) Yes-yes, Nelly. I'll be perfectly fine.

BORIS. Come on, Nelly, let's get to that yummy *cockroach*!

NELLY. (*Correcting him.*) "*Pot roast*"! (*Exits with* BORIS; *the moment they are gone,* DRACULA *rises up into view from behind wingback of chaise [see SPECIAL EFFECTS] and gazes hungrily down on* MINA, *who is relaxing there with her eyes closed.*)

DRACULA. I thought they'd *never* leave!

MINA. (*Startled, springs to her feet, whirls to face him.*) You! But how did you—where did you—?!

DRACULA. From the moment I saw your lovely face, I knew you must be mine. That is the reason I came here tonight.

MINA. (*Backs from him to point below sofa.*) Saw *my* face? *Before* you came here tonight?

DRACULA. Jonathan Harker carried your photograph with him on his journey. I saw it in his room one night.

MINA. Jonathan! Where is he? What have you *done* with him?

DRACULA. (*Moves toward her, slowly.*) Nothing that cannot be *un*done . . . if I have your willing cooperation.

MINA. You would use that against me? My love for Jonathan? You would force me to your will by threatening his life?

DRACULA. (*Reaches out, gently grasps her upper arms.*) There is nothing I would not do to have you as my own.

MINA. Your hands—they're like ice—yet your eyes burn with golden fires—!

DRACULA. (*MUSIC intros and he draws her into his arms, and—dancing her unresistingly in a slow, strange dance—he sings.*)

DON'T BE AFRAID! BELONG TO ME!
WE CAN'T EVADE OUR DESTINY!
LOOK IN MY EYES! YOU CANNOT FLEE!
YOU REALIZE YOU'RE MEANT TO BE
WITH ME ETERNALLY!
COME, SATISFY MY ENSLAVING CRAVING!
RELIEVE THE RAVING HUNGER IN MY HEART!
IT'S TIME TO START!

(*The dance slows to a standstill, and she can only stare helplessly into his eyes as he finishes.*)

NOW YOU SHALL SURELY FIND DARK DELIGHT!
DON'T DECLINE . . .! YOU ARE MINE TONIGHT!
(*As final weird trilling of music sounds, he bends her back, his mouth going to her throat, his cloak enfolding the two of them, and she shuts her eyes and leans her head back as his mouth descends upon her—and then* BORIS *rushes in* U.L., *a napkin tucked into the neck of his blouse, and lopes down toward them [they are in area between desk and mirror], on.*)

BORIS. Master! Van Helsing is coming! You must fly!

DRACULA. (*Thrusts* MINA *from him toward wall, shouts to her.*) Be patient, my darling! I shall return for you within the hour! (*Starts to rush toward* U.C., *but halts as* VAN *dashes in* U.L., *sees him, and rushes toward him, on.*)

VAN. Dracula! Stand where you are! (*He takes something from his pocket and thrusts it toward* DRACULA, *who staggers back, rolling up in his cloak almost into a ball into the angle of desk and wall—and then there is a puff of smoke, and a huge bat flies out of the smoke, soars* U. *and vanishes into the night* U.C. *[see SPECIAL EFFECTS]; simultaneous with* VAN's *shout,* MINA *has screamed and swooned,* BORIS *catching her as she starts to slide down wall, so that bat's exit is between those two and the onrushing* VAN.) The monster has escaped! How is Mina? (*As* VAN *goes to her,* SAM, SOPHIE, BUBU *and* NELLY *all rush in* U.L., *converging on them as* VAN *carries* MINA *to sofa and lays her down there, newcomers all adlibbing things like "What's happened?", "What was that scream?" etc.*) Be quiet, all of you! She's all right. I was—in time!

SOPHIE. In time for what?

BUBU. What's going on here?

BORIS. Well, Count Dracula was here trying to take Mina as his bride, but Van Helsing showed up, and the count turned into a bat and flew away! (*Newcomers have simply stared at* BORIS *during this recital; then, after two beats,* SAM *turns to* VAN.)

SAM. I *told* you he was nuts!

NELLY. What *really* happened?

VAN. Precisely what he said. If I had not had *this*—Mina would even now be gone off into the night with that foul fiend! (*On demonstrative pronoun, has extended object.*)

NELLY. (*Leans over it.*) What *is* that?

VAN. A clove of garlic! Vampires cannot *bear* to have it near them!

NELLY. (*Making a face and recoiling.*) Who could *blame* them! Pee-*yoo*!

VAN. You've got to believe me, all of you! Mina is in dreadful danger! We must all unite in a combined effort to overcome our monstrous foe!

SOPHIE. What foe?

VAN. (*Rages.*) Because I *said* so!

BUBU. But Van—surely you're mistaken! It couldn't have been the count you saw! He was strolling in the garden, and I'll *swear* he never passed back through the house to come up here . . . ?!

VAN. Can I not make you all understand?! What are doors to a vampire? Or walls? Or staircases? They mean nothing to him—nothing!

SAM. Steady, man, steady! You're talking nonsense! After all, this *is* the Nineteenth Century!

MINA. (*Abruptly moans;* OTHERS *instantly look her way; she writhes, blinks, and suddenly sits up.*) Oh! What's happened?! Why am I here on this sofa? The count—is he gone?!

SOPHIE. He was never here, my dear.

BUBU. You're just imagining things.

NELLY. There's no one here but *normal* people!

BORIS. (*Scuffs foot on carpet, flattered.*) Aw shucks, Nelly!

MINA. (*Gets to her feet.*) But I could have sworn—! It all seemed so real! He was here—he took me in his arms—he sang the strangest song to me—and we danced—and then—and then—everything seemed to dissolve—there were only his eyes—his bright burning eyes—!

SOPHIE. Darling, you've just had a bad dream.

NELLY. Lightheaded, you are, from having no dinner.

BUBU. Yes, of course, that's it!

SAM. You really should eat something, dear.

VAN. Stop it! All of you, stop it! Mina is in mortal peril! Can't I make you believe me?!

SAM. But Van Helsing—what you are suggesting is sorcery—black magic—idiotic superstition!

VAN. But don't you see?! That attitude is precisely what he's *counting* on! Blindness! Blindness until it's too late! The only way I can *prove* my contention is to *let* him take Mina!

SOPHIE. Doctor, you're overwrought!

BUBU. Maybe you should have a drink to calm your nerves.

SAM. Maybe we should *all* have something! It's been a rather unsettling evening! . . . Nelly—?

NELLY. Thanks, I could *use* a snort! (*Starts for liquor.*)

SAM. I *mean*—would you fix *us* all a drink?! (*She stops, hands on hips, and glares at him; he wilts.*) *And* one for yourself, of course. (*Mollified, she moves toward liquor again.*)

VAN. Not very subservient, *is* she!

SAM. She *used* to be.

SOPHIE. But of late, dear, I do detect a definite difference in her diffident deference!

NELLY. What would everybody like?

VAN. I suppose a drink *would* be a good idea, at that! I'll have a scotch and soda—with a maximum of scotch, and just a mini-soda!

BORIS. (*Instantly wild-eyed.*) *Mini-soda*! (*Same reaction from ALL OTHERS as at last song of his, as* BORIS *happily goes into his vocal aberration.*)

A STATE THAT I THOUGHT WAS SO VERY NICE!
IF YOU'LL TAKE MY ADVICE,
YOU'LL TURN YOUR FACES TO
THAT PLACE SO SUPER-GREAT . . .
CALLED MIN-NE-SO-TA STATE . . .!
            (*Same tempo-acceleration, etc., during:*)
WINONA HAS A LOT OF GREAT TO-
BOGGANING AND IN MANKATO
EV'RYONE'S A SORRY CYNIC
'CAUSE THEY GOT NO MAYO CLINIC,
AND ST. PAUL FOLKS TURN UNCOUTH
IF YOU PRAISE MINNEAPOLIS,
AND BOTH OF THEM ARE MAD AT DULUTH!
(*MAD DANCE for EVERYBODY, as before, ending with ALL back in kickoff-positions, calm and serene instantly.*)

SOPHIE. Really, Mister Renfield, I *do* wish you wouldn't *do* that!

NELLY. It beats watching him eat spiders!

VAN. We're getting off the track! Don't you understand?! We have to *destroy* this monster before *he* destroys *Mina*!

MINA. (*Clutches him.*) Oh, yes, yes! We must! But how?! He is so strong, so swift, so powerful!

VAN. We drive a wooden stake through his heart!

NELLY. What do you mean, "*we*"?!

VAN. All right, all right, *I* drive the stake through his heart. A stake of one of the hardest woods there is!

SAM. What wood is that?

VAN. The wood of the ash tree.

BUBU. Ash? What's so special about ash?

VAN. Well, according to baseball fans, it's the *only* wood to use for *bats*—!

BUBU. But Van—are you *sure* it isn't all nonsense? I mean—vampires—in this day and age!

SAM. Yes, it's probably only a mental aberration on the part of Count Dracula. He merely *thinks* he's a vampire, is all. I'm sure that, given the opportunity, I could cure him via scientific analysis. I'd be willing to bet on it!

VAN. (*Hopefully.*) How *big* a bet—?

SAM. Oh, I didn't mean *money!*

MINA. Then what? You've got to bet him *something*, Father!

BUBU. I've got it! Bet him *my* hand in *marriage!*

SOPHIE. But Bubu—*Sam* has no say-so in *your* wedding.

NELLY. You're not even a member of his family!

VAN. Well, that's *one* point in her favor!

SAM. All right, I'll *do* it! Bubu shall be the bet!

BUBU. Good, then it's all settled! (*To* SAM.) You bet your Bubu—

BUBU. (*To* VAN.) And you bet your ash!

VAN. But I warn you all—we must be dreadfully careful! By day, Count Dracula is helpless as a kitten, and easily approached—but during the hours of night, no power on earth can destroy him—so long as darkness rules the land, he can render normal human beings helpless with a gesture—until the rise of the sun in the morning, he can do anything he chooses without fear of failure—!

NELLY. But—it *is* night time—!

SOPHIE. And darkness *does* rule the land—!

BUBU. And the sun won't be up for *hours* yet—!

BORIS. Say! You're right! In which case— (*Gestures dramatically up toward* U.C. *doorway.*) Heeeeere's *Dracky!* (DRACULA *instantly steps into view on balcony [see SPECIAL RECOMMENDATIONS]*)

DRACULA. (*Raises his hands imperiously.*) Stand where you are, all of you! (*ALL but* BORIS *freeze as if turned to stone.*)

BORIS. (*Scurrying halfway to him.*) Oh, Master, you do things *so* nicely!

DRACULA. I don't understand . . . why aren't *you* paralyzed by my power?!

BORIS. (*Shrugs.*) Like the doctor said—it only works on *nor-*

mal human beings! (*Scurries a few steps closer to him.*) Is it time? Have you come to make me immortal as you are? Will you keep all your promises to me at last?

DRACULA. Uh . . . sure, kid, sure! Look—I got an idea—why don't you go throw a few things into a bag, hurry back here, and we'll head for my castle and wrap matters up, okay?

BORIS. (*Elated.*) Wowee, *yes*, Master! (*Lopes off* U.R., *during string of.*) Oh boy-o-boy-o-boy-o-boy—! (*Saying enough to get him off.*)

DRACULA. (*The moment he is gone, strikes stance, makes one-arm's-length "magnetizing" motion with his hand, on:*) Meeeee-na! . . . Come to me! Now is our moment of triumph! Come!

MINA. (*Slowly takes a step toward him, though OTHERS re-main frozen where they are; then she stops.*) I cannot! I dare not! I am too afraid!

DRACULA. You would not fear if you but knew the unearthly blisses to which I summon you . . .! (*MUSIC intros and he sings.*)

COME INTO MY WORLD OF ENDLESS NIGHT!
COME INTO A WORLD OF STRANGE DELIGHT!
COME AND FIND THE LOVE THAT'S WAITING FOR
YOU FOREVERMORE!
FLOAT THROUGH THE VELVET DARKNESS BY
MY SIDE!
COME NOW! BECOME MY BRIDE! I WON'T BE DENIED!
  (MINA *will move like a somnambulist toward him, now.*)
YOU MUST BE MY LOVE!
  MINA.
MY LOVE, YES, I'LL COME!
  DRACULA.
COME INTO MY—
  MINA.
INTO YOUR—
  DRACULA/MINA.
WORLD OF ENDLESS NIGHT!
TO A MOONLIT WORLD OF STRANGE DELIGHT!
EVERMORE TO BREATHLESSLY PURSUE
DEATHLESS JOY WITH YOU!
(*She has reached him, now, and stands beside him, facing out
    front, his cloaked arm across her shoulder.*)
HASTENING HEARTBEATS HUNGRILY DECREE
THAT THIS MUST COME TO BE!

DRACULA.
OH, COME NOW WITH ME! SHARE MY DELIGHT!
BOTH.
EVER TO BE THERE IN THE NIGHT!
DRACULA.
SEVER FOREVER YOUR TIES TO THE WAKING WORLD . . .
MINA.
I'LL FORSAKE MY WORLD . . .
DRACULA.
COME, PARTAKE MY WORLD . . .!
(*Then off through* U.R. *we hear, louder and louder:*)
BORIS. Master! Master! Ready or not, here I come! All dressed up and ready to go! Don't leave without me!
DRACULA. (*Speaking the moment he hears* BORIS's *first words, so that* BORIS's *speech is still being heard over:*) Quickly, my darling, we must fly! (*Swings her up onto balcony rail, springs up beside her.*) Take my hand, and let's go!
MINA. Go where?! It's a four-hundred-foot drop to jagged rocks!
DRACULA. (*Clasps her hand.*) Keep hold of my hand and you will be safe!
MINA. Are you sure?
DRACULA. No. But there's one way to find out—! (*Springs from sight over rail, pulling* MINA *with him.*)
MINA. (*Out of view beyond rail.*) Helllllp—! (*An instant later,* BORIS *rushes on,* U.R., *dressed as we last saw him, but now wearing a Tyrolean hat, carrying a small suitcase in one hand, and supporting the over-the-shoulder strap of a large bag of golf clubs slung on his back with the other; as he rushes to the rail, paralysis leaves* OTHERS, *and all but* VAN *stagger and sway, dazed, but* VAN *rushes to rail to look out into the night from beside* BORIS; *all this happens during:*)
BORIS. (*As he gets to rail.*) Master! Wait! Come back here! You promised!
VAN. (*Arrives at rail just as* BORIS *finishes.*) Look there! Out in the night, riding the black winds of darkness, a gigantic bat, carrying Mina off toward the castle of Dracula!
SAM. Now-now, Van Helsing, what you need is a couple of aspirin and a good night's sleep.
VAN. (*Whirls to face into room.*) You fools! Do you *still* refuse to believe me?!

SOPHIE. Well, Doctor, it *is* a bit farfetched!

NELLY. Giant bats, indeed!

BUBU. Van, darling, you *are* asking us to swallow quite a tall story—!

VAN. There's no time to argue! (*Clutches* BORIS.) Renfield! Can *you* lead me to the monster's lair?!

BORIS. What?! Approach a vampire's castle by crossing a swamp on foot in the middle of the night with a thunderstorm coming up? Only a *crazy* man would try it!

VAN. You *are* a crazy man!

BORIS. Then what are we *waiting* for!? (BORIS *and* VAN *dash out* U.L..)

SAM. Of all things! (*Moves down toward front right of sofa.*)

SOPHIE. Utter tommyrot! (*Moves down toward front left of sofa.*)

BUBU. Such silly carryings-on! (*Moves down between chaise and fireplace.*)

NELLY. And at such an ungodly hour of night! (*Moves down near desk.*) (*MUSIC intros, and—none realizing the double meaning in each individual line of the four-line verse that starts this final song of the act—they sing.*)

SAM.

THE WALKING DEAD ARE NOTHING BUT ROT!

SOPHIE.

THEIR MOLDERING GRAVEYARD IS JUST A LOT
OF JUNK!

NELLY.

THE OPEN GRAVE IS AN OVERT PLOT!

BUBU.

AND A COFFIN FOR A BED IS THE PLAINEST BUNK!

(*As ALL proceed into the refrain, the pattern is this: The melody and delivery are upbeat and jolly, except for each of* NELLY'*s lines, during which the OTHERS all smile very uneasily, then recover for subsequent lines, only to lose their courage each new time she chimes in; on final line of the song, of course, all faces of all four are models of mindless terror.*)

SAM.

NO PERSON OF INTELLIGENCE BELIEVES SUCH
SILLY TALES!
WE GRASP THE FACTS WHERE OTHERS
SIMPLY GROPE!

SOPHIE.

IMAGINE FINDING MENACE IN THE WIND EACH
TIME IT WAILS!

ALL.

IT'S A STUPID SUPERSTITION!

NELLY.

. . . WE HOPE!

BUBU.

IT'S HARD TO SHARE THE NOTION THAT WITH EV'RY
FALL OF NIGHT
MAD MONSTERS THROUGH THE MIST MAY SLYLY
SLINK!

ALL.

TO FEEL A FIEND BEHIND YOU AS YOU'RE TURNING
OUT THE LIGHT
IS A STUPID SUPERSTITION!

NELLY.

. . . WE THINK!

SAM.

WE LAUGH AT NERVOUS VILLAGERS AND SCOFF
AT ALL THEIR FEARS—

SOPHIE.

THAT GRUESOME THINGS MAY GRAB US UNAWARES!

BUBU.

DESPITE THOSE BEDTIME WARNINGS SOMETHING
WHISPERS IN OUR EARS—

ALL.

WE GO MERRILY UPSTAIRS!

NELLY.

WHILE WHIMPERING OUR PRAYERS!

BUBU.

WHY SHOULD WE SHOOT THE BOLTS BECAUSE A
WOLF BEGINS TO BARK?

SOPHIE.

WHY PANIC AS THE DAYLIGHT FADES AWAY?

SAM.

HOW FOOLISH TO SUPPOSE THERE'S FRIGHTFUL
DANGER IN THE DARK!

ALL.

IT'S A STUPID SUPERSTITION!

NELLY.

. . . WE PRAY!

SOPHIE.

WHENEVER AN EVENT OCCURS THAT CANNOT BE
EXPLAINED—
    SAM.
MISGUIDED PEASANTS TEND TO LOSE THEIR HEADS!
    BUBU.
THEY BABBLE OF THE BEASTLY THINGS THE
DARKNESS HAS UNCHAINED—
    ALL.
BUT WE RIDICULE THEIR DREADS!
    NELLY.
FROM UNDERNEATH OUR BEDS!
    SAM.
A MAN WHO TURNS INTO A BAT UNDOUBTEDLY LAYS
BARE
SOME NATURAL [NATCH-RAL] LAW THAT'S NOT YET
UNDERSTOOD!
    SOPHIE.
SO THOUGH SUCH HORRID STORIES GIVE THE
SIMPLETONS A SCARE—
    BUBU.
WE WOULD BALK AT EXHIBITION—
    BUBU/SOPHIE.
OF SUCH NERVOUS PREMONITION—
    BUBU/SOPHIE/SAM.
IT'S A STUPID SUPERSTITION . . .
    ALL FOUR. (*Each rapping once-per-syllable on nearest object:
desk, right endtable, left endtable and mantel.*) *Knock on wood*!
(*and as they sustain final note with faces of dread and despera-
tion, and lively music plays out to its giddy finish—*)

THE CURTAIN FALLS

End of Act One

ACT TWO

Several hours later, shortly before dawn. Curtain-rise finds
SAM, *in pajamas, robe and slippers, poker in hand, prodding
the dying logs in the fireplace.* BUBU, SOPHIE *and* NELLY
*are seated side by side on the sofa; each is in a long white
nightgown and white peignoir, looking almost identical, except that* NELLY *still wears her maid's cap. After a moment,*
SAM *replaces poker in hearthside rack and turns to face
group on sofa.*

SAM. Fire's about out. I suppose we should all go to bed.

SOPHIE. But we can't lock up until Renfield and Doctor Van
Helsing return.

NELLY. But what if they *never* return?!

BUBU. Don't say such things, Nelly! Surely they're all right.
They *have* to be all right!

SAM. And why do you say that?

BUBU. Well, for one thing, Van is the first unmarried doctor
I've ever met. How many chances like that does a girl get? (VAN
and BORIS, *looking weary, enter* U.L., BORIS *still with hat, suitcase and clubs.*)

SAM. Van Helsing! Renfield! (WOMEN *come to their feet and
turn.*)

BUBU. (*Rushing to him.*) Van! You're alive! You're safe! I
can't tell you how pleased I am!

BORIS. What about *me*?

BUBU. Oh, *you* can tell him how pleased you are.

SOPHIE. (*As* BORIS, VAN *and* BUBU *come down below sofa.*)
Did you have any luck?

VAN. Regrettably — no. We wandered in the swamp for hours.
It was as though an evil spell was upon the place — no matter
how many times we tried to reach Dracula's castle, it seemed to
elude us, to turn us about, to lose us in a maze of water and moss
and mist!

NELLY. But — if you've been wandering through the
swamp — why aren't your trousers soggy?

VAN. (*Guiltily.*) Well — we didn't want to go in *too* deep . . .!

BORIS. (*Just as guiltily.*) No point in catching cold . . .!

VAN. (*Abruptly.*) Good grief! What are you ladies wearing?!

SOPHIE. Why — just long white nightgowns and long white
peignoirs.

35

VAN. Are you crazy?! Don't you know that when a monster carries a woman off in his arms, she is almost *invariably* wearing a long white trailing garment?

WOMEN. (*Out front, in a unified dreamy sigh.*) Do we ever!

SAM. (*Sits suddenly on chaise's lower edge, facing sofa.*) Sophie, what are you saying?!

SOPHIE. (*Only slightly guilty.*) Well, mostly it was Bubu's idea.

NELLY. She said it was a sort of theatrical tradition.

BUBU. Because that's exactly what it *is*! (*MUSIC intros, and she stands and sings.*)
AS YEAR SUCCEEDED YEAR, AND MY
THEATRICAL CAREER
PROGRESSED FROM CARRYING A SPEAR TO BEING
ALL THE RAGE,
I MOVED TO CAVIAR FROM CRULLER BY LEARNING
NOTHING'S DULLER
THAN WEARING THE WRONG COLOR WHEN YOU
ENTER ON A STAGE . . .
    (*Primly polite.*)
THE LADY IN GREEN MUST BE EVER SO SERENE
MOVING CALMLY THROUGH EACH SCENE
OF THE PLAY . . .
    (*With raucous growl and sexy movements.*)
BUT AS THE LADY IN WHITE, THE LADY IN WHITE,
YOU CAN GET CARRIED AWAY!

SOPHIE. (*Rises to stand beside* BUBU, *for:*)
THE LADY IN BLUE, SHE COULD BORE YOU
THROUGH AND THROUGH,
HER POLITENESS IS TOO-TOO *DISTINGUÉ* . . .
    (*Same shift to growl, dance.*)
BUT AS THE LADY IN WHITE, THE LADY IN WHITE,
YOU CAN GET CARRIED AWAY!

NELLY. (*Rises, and all three strut right as she sings.*)
THE ACTRESS WEARING TAN NEVER WINDS UP
WITH A MAN!

BUBU.
THE GAL IN BROWN IS ALWAYS FORTY AND FAT!
  (*They are near desk, now, and reverse direction on:*)
SOPHIE.
THE ONE IN CERISE PLAYS AN UNIMPORTANT NIECE!
(*Midway back to sofa, trio faces front, leans front with hands
  on knees to complete the phrase.*)

WOMEN.
BUT SHOWY, SNOWY WHITE IS WHERE THE ACTION
IS AT!
>   (*Continue strut back sofaward during.*)
NELLY.
THE LADY IN RED DRIVES A MAN OUT OF HIS HEAD,
BUT SHE'LL NEVER THROW A WEDDING BOUQUET!
(*Trio now puts hands on hips, moves D. in hip-thrust stripper-steps [left foot and left hip, then right foot and right hip, etc.] toward audience on.*)
WOMEN.
'CAUSE FOR THE LADY IN WHITE HE'D MUCH
RATHER FIGHT!
HER PROSPECTS ARE DELIGHTFULLY GAY!
(*Fairly frenzied pseudo-burlesque movements now to end of song—overhead arm-waving, swaying, hip-swinging, etc.*)
SO ANY DAY, ANY NIGHT, BE THE LADY IN WHITE!
THE TWEEDY LADY IN SHADY DARK GRAY
HE WON'T BE COURTIN'!
BUT IF YOU'RE LOOKING PURE AS THE DAY
HE'LL COME A-SNORTIN'!
SO DON'T WEAR CLOTHES WHOSE COLOR IS VARIED,
'CAUSE WHITE'S SO RIGHT FOR GETTING
GIRLS MARRIED,
AND THEN AND THERE YOU'RE GONNA GET
CARRIED AWAY!
(*At finish, they are in original position before sofa, and they sit sedately down, and demurely cross each of their left legs over the right on final beat.*)

SAM. (*Stands.*) Never mind all that tommyrot! What's become of *Mina*?!

VAN. Sam, you *saw* the monster *snatch* her!

SOPHIE. But we might merely have imagined the entire incident.

VAN. What?! Then tell me this: If she wasn't snatched, where *is* she? (*Then ALL look up as MINA—garbed identically to the rest of the women—enters U.R.; her face is chalk-white, her eyes over-mascaraed, and lipstick dark red, and she has a wide white bandage about her throat.*)

MINA. What's going on? You woke me out of a sound sleep!

SAM. (*To VAN.*) Does that answer your question?

SOPHIE. What did we tell you!

BUBU. Perfectly safe and sound!

NELLY. But why has she got a bandage about her throat?

MINA. (*Who has been moving* D., *stops, a hand going briefly to the bandage.*) What? Oh, this! It's—it's nothing. I . . . cut myself shaving!

VAN. (*Moving toward her.*) Shaving what? You don't have a beard! . . . Do you?

MINA. (*Tries to brazen it out.*) Uh—well—not any *more*! That's *why* I was shaving!

VAN. (*Reaches out.*) I should very much like to *see* that cut . . .!

MINA. (*Evading his grasp, rushes down to* SAM, *on:*) Oh, Father! Make him stop! Send him away! I don't like him! He upsets me dreadfully!

VAN. All I wanted was one quick peek!

MINA. No! I won't let you!

SAM. (*Holds her in his arms, uncertainly.*) But surely, Mina, it wouldn't do any harm to let him have a *look*, would it?

SOPHIE. After all, darling, the man *is* a *doctor*—!

MINA. (*Defensively.*) Well, so is Father! If someone must look, I'd rather it were he! (*Plops herself down on chaise, feet out in front of her, folding her arms defiantly.*)

SAM. (*Between fireplace and chaise.*) Well, that seems fair enough. (*Leans forward, takes peek beneath bandage on left side of her throat, reacts, straightens.*) Mina—did you say—*shaving*?

BUBU. She certainly did.

NELLY. We all heard her.

SOPHIE. Why?

SAM. Because—it isn't a *cut*—it seems, rather, to be—*punctures*!

VAN. (*Now down between sofa and chaise.*) Aha! Two small punctures? About an inch apart?

SAM. Well, actually, there are *three*.

VAN. (*Reacts.*) *Three*?! Then Dracula must be even *more* of a monster than I had *imagined*! . . . Doctor Seward, are you absolutely *sure*?

SAM. I'd stake my reputation as a doctor on it!

BORIS. That's not saying much.

MINA. (*Comes angrily to her feet.*) Enough of all this! I'm very tired, and unusually weak, and somewhat paler than normal, and I think I'll go to bed! (*Starts moving toward* U.R., *pushing* VAN *aside en route.*)

SAM. Splendid idea! We could all use some rest! (*Trails after* MINA.) Coming, Sophie?

SOPHIE. (*Moving around right end of sofa to join his exit.*) Yes, it's been a very long night!

NELLY. You can say that again! (*Starts up after departing* SEWARDS.) Aren't *you* coming, Miss Padoop?

BUBU. Uh . . . no . . . not just yet. I think I'll stay and chat with the doctor for a bit. (MINA, SAM *and* SOPHIE *will exit* U.R. *just before:*)

NELLY. Suit yourself. (*Beckons to* BORIS, *who has been standing uncertainly midway between sofa and* U.R..) Come along, Renfield, it's time to lock you up for the night.

BORIS. (*Moving reluctantly after her.*) But I'll *only* mysteriously get *out* again, like I *always* do!

NELLY. (*Leading him off* U.R.) Rules are rules. What you do after you're safely in your cell is your own business. (*They exit.*)

VAN. (*Sinks down at left end of sofa, disconsolate.*) I feel so helpless. Why can I get no one to believe me?

BUBU. (*Moves toward him, will sit beside him during.*) Maybe if you didn't make such loony claims all the time. They *are* rather hard to credit . . .

VAN. (*Turns, takes her hands.*) Ah, Bubu, if I could only convince *you*—that would be *something*, at any rate!

BUBU. I'd *love* to be convinced, Van—but you talk so *nutty*! Let's talk about something else. Tell me all about your work.

VAN. (*Shrugs, speaks offhandedly.*) Nothing much to tell. Usual sort of thing. Driving wooden stakes through hearts . . . incinerating coffins . . . always carrying a pocketful of garlic . . . dragging the undead out to see the sunrise . . . just a run-of-the-mill medical occupation.

BUBU. (*Moves closer to him, in a cuddly fashion.*) Of course it is, dearest! Now let's talk about—us!

VAN. (*Startled.*) Us? What do you mean, us?

BUBU. (*Practically.*) Us. You and me. Together. Both. Hand-in-hand, facing the future together, man and wife . . .!

VAN. Bubu! You don't know what you're saying! Do you have any notion what marriage to a man in my line of work would mean?! (*MUSIC intros and he sings.*)

I FEAR I'D MAKE A HORRID HUSBAND.
YOU'D BE A MOST UNHAPPY BRIDE.
I COULD NOT ASK YOU, DEAR, TO SHARE MY WORK
WHERE PERILS LURK ON EV'RY SIDE!

YET COULD I BEAR IT IF I WAS BANNED
FROM MY TRUE WORK FOR LOVE OF YOU?
NO-NO! I'M FORCED TO SPURN YOU,
FOR, MY DEAR, I KNOW I'D TURN YOU
OFF WITH EV'RY COFFIN BARBEQUE!
   BUBU.
HOW VERY KINDLY YOUR FEELINGS ARE!
BUT I DON'T MIND LIAISONS WITH A MAN
WHO'S SO BIZARRE!
SO EVEN—
(BOTH *rise to their feet, still holding hands.*)
   VAN/BUBU.
THOUGH I/YOU MIGHT MAKE A HORRID HUSBAND
THERE'S SOMETHING TO BE SAID FOR GLOOM!
FOR THOUGH I/YOU WANDER FAR FROM
YOUR/MY EMBRACE,
I'LL/YOU'LL SEE YOUR/MY FACE IN EV'RY TOMB!
   BUBU. (*Embraces him, her cheek against his chest.*)
I'D TURN YOU TO A TORRID HUSBAND
WHENEVER YOU CAME HOME TO ME . . .
   VAN/BUBU. (*He resignedly embraces her, they sit, and* BOTH
finish out front.)
SO, WHAT THE HELL,
THOUGH I/YOU AM/ARE SEL-
DOM HERE TO SEE,
LET'S TRY TO REL-
ISH ENDLESS LOVE . . .
INFREQUENTLY!
(*At song's end, they are about to kiss, but are interrupted by a
   LOUD THUNDERCRASH, which brings both of them to
   their feet.*)
   BUBU. Seems to be a storm coming up.
   VAN. I don't like this! Thunderstorms make marvelous
weather for weirdos!
   BUBU. Stop being such a spook! Let's chat about our wed-
ding!
   VAN. How can I concentrate on bliss when I'm so worried
about Mina?
   BUBU. Mina! Always Mina! Mina this, Mina that! Sometimes
I wonder if you don't care more for her than you do for me!
   VAN. I'm only concerned for her safety! Bubu, are you blind?
Haven't you noticed how *strange* Mina's conduct has become?

(*Then amid another THUNDERCRASH,* MINA *enters* U.R., *steps quickly to* U.C. *doorway and looks out.*)

MINA. (*With awe in her voice.*) What a night! Black skies — icy rain — gale-force winds —! (*Then, to twosome, brightly.*) I think I'll go out for a stroll! (*Gives a whoop of glee, hitches up her skirts, and gallops off* U.L..)

BUBU. (*After a pause, turns to face* VAN *again.*) Strange in what way? (VAN *does a double-take at her, and opens his mouth to speak, but stops as* SOPHIE, SAM, BORIS *and* NELLY *all come rushing in* U.R. *and down toward sofa, on.*)

SOPHIE. Mina's not in her room!

SAM. Her door is wide open!

NELLY. Her bed hasn't been slept in!

BORIS. And her galoshes are gone!

SOPHIE. She doesn't *own* any galoshes!

BORIS. (*Shrugs.*) Well, I looked in her closet, and *somebody's* galoshes aren't there!

SAM. I must be cracking up. That almost makes sense.

NELLY. I hope she hasn't gone out-of-doors! Not on a night like this!

BUBU. She could catch pneumonia!

VAN. If something doesn't catch her first!

SAM. Oh, will you cease that foolish balderdash about monsters and such!

VAN. But we've got to *save* her! She's *already* been bitten by a vampire *once*!

BORIS. Once-and-a-*half*! (*When* ALL *look his way.*) Well, you *said* there were *three* punctures —!

SOPHIE. And what does it matter *how* many times she's been bitten?

VAN. The first time makes her his slave . . . the second time renders her too weak to run away . . . and the third —

OTHERS. Yes? . . . *Yes*?

VAN. The third assault upon Mina will turn her into the same dreaded thing that he himself must forever be!

SOPHIE. *Hungarian*?!

VAN. Look —! You've *all* seen signs of his supernatural nature — those wilted flowers — his missing reflection in the mirror — the way he came upstairs without passing through the dining room — What does it take to *convince* you?!

BUBU. Van, I think the nub of the problem is that there's no way you can convince us *Count Dracula* is a vampire until you first convince us there are even *such things* as vampires!

VAN. Aha! Of course! That's *it*! (*Grabs* BUBU *by upper arms, kisses her hard and quickly, then releases her and rushes to bookshelf over desk.*) Maybe if you see for yourself in black-and-white—! (*Grabs volume off shelf, runs to* SAM *with it.*)

SAM. (*Stares stupidly at book.*) See *what* in black-and-white?

VAN. The truth about *vampires*! Maybe you don't believe *me*—but you've *got* to believe the encyclopedia! (SAM *sits reluctantly at center of sofa, with* SOPHIE *sitting at his left and* BUBU *at his right, while* BORIS *and* NELLY *take up respective leaning-in-to-look places at right and left arms of sofa, on which they sit, while* VAN *moves to a spot* U. *of table and sofa directly behind* SAM, *leaning across the table to see the open pages of the book along with the others; this all occurs over next three speeches.*)

SOPHIE. Oh, Sam, do you think it *is* true—?

SAM. Well, we'll see for ourselves soon enough!

BUBU. And if Van has been right all along—what do we do then?

SAM. (*Opening book, starting to page through it.*) Hush, my child. First let us find the proper page . . . (*Spots something, stops, smiles, and points it out.*) Look, Sophie! The Grand Canal! Remember our vacation there?

VAN. That's *Venice*! Doctor Seward, you went too far!

SOPHIE. Sam! You promised you'd never tell!

VAN. In the book, in the book! Turn back a few pages!

SAM. (*Doing so.*) Oh, yes. Sorry . . . Ah, here we are—"Vampires" . . . (*Starts to read, mumbling incoherently as he does so, and attempts to turn the page, but* SOPHIE *stops him.*)

SOPHIE. Not so fast, Sam—I got a little behind!

VAN. (*At his wit's end.*) Not from *this* angle!

BUBU. *Van*!

SOPHIE. How dare you!

SAM. Really, Van Helsing—!

NELLY. (*Points at* BORIS *as she speaks to* VAN.) Even this disgusting *lunatic* has better manners than *that*!

BORIS. Why, thank you, Nelly . . . I think.

VAN. I apologize, I apologize! Now, *read*! And be quick about it, for at every passing moment your daughter is in increasing danger at the hands of this insidiously cruel and callous foreigner!

BORIS. (*Springs to his feet in wild-eyed glee.*) *Callous*

foreigner! (OTHERS *will react, freeze in apprehensive shock, and do all the usual business including the post-lyric mad gypsy dance, during his song.*)
A STATE THAT I THOUGHT WAS SO VERY NICE!
IF YOU'LL TAKE MY ADVICE,
YOU'LL TURN YOUR FACES TO
THE PLACES YOU MAY STAY,
IN CAL-I-FOR-NI-AY . . .!
  (*Same slow start going into fast finish.*)
THERE'S ALTA LOMA, MONTEREY, A
FUNNY SMELL THROUGHOUT LA BREA,
EL CAMINO, SANTA CRUZ, AND
CITRUS COLLEGE IN AZUSA,
SAN FRANCISCO'S EAGER GUIDES,
AND SACRAMENTO, FRESNO, BAKERSFIELD,
AND CUCAMONGA, BESIDES!
  (*Mad dance;* ALL *end up where they began.*)
 VAN. (*Leaning on table, trying to catch his breath.*) Now, if we can . . . just get back to . . . the encyclopedia—? (*Then* MINA *enters* U.L., *weakly, dragging her feet, stopping just inside archway and leaning back upon lower edge of it for support; her face is now the color of whitewash, eyes completely encircled with deepest black, and her lips red as flame.*)
 NELLY. (*The first to spot her.*) Look! It's Miss Mina! (OTHERS *turn, look, but do not move from places.*)
 SAM. There, Van Helsing, what did I tell you!
 SOPHIE. Perfectly normal—
 BUBU. And safe and sound!
 VAN. Are you all *crazy*?! Just *look* at her! She's two-thirds on her way to Vampireville *already*!
 MINA. (*Straightens with dignity, makes negating gesture.*) Nonsense! (*Flowers on pier table wilt instantly [see SPECIAL EFFECTS];* OTHERS *react.*)
 SOPHIE. Sam, did you see *that*?!
 BUBU. You mean—everything Van has told us is *true*?!
 MINA. (*Steps just off edge of raised area, moves toward mirror.*) Stop listening to his lies! He should be locked up with all the other lunatics! I'm perfectly fine, as always, and any fool can see I'm still my old sweet self! (*Looks at her image in mirror, starts to pat at her hair—and her image slowly fades till we can barely see it [see SPECIAL EFFECTS]; she reacts slightly.*) Nelly, when was the last time you dusted this mirror! I can hardly see a

thing in it! (*Moves* U., *exits with slight stagger* U.R.)

SAM. (*As* ALL *move tentatively* U. *a bit.*) Good heavens! Did you see that?!

SOPHIE. Those flowers—!

BUBU. And that reflection—!

NELLY. You don't suppose that—everything Doctor Van Helsing told us is *true*?!

VAN. Of course it's true! And we've got to *help* Mina, *now*!

SAM. How?

VAN. We rush to her room, tie her to the bed, and rub her body from head to toe with garlic!

BORIS. Whee! Can *I* help, huh, can I, huh?!

SAM. *You* are going back to your *cell*!

NELLY. It won't do any good. He always gets right out again.

SAM. (*To* NELLY.) And *you* are going to lock things up for the night, so that ghastly creature can't come back here!

NELLY. (*Ceases her place in the general exodus toward* U.R.) But what good will it do? Locked doors don't stop vampires!

SAM. (*Icily.*) They will at least go to show him that we highly disapprove of his conduct! . . . Come along, all of you! We've got to get Mina garlicked down for the night!

NELLY. (*As* OTHERS *exit.*) She's gonna smell worse than that *pot roast*, poor kid!

VAN. (*One of the last to exit.*) Aha! The pot roast was prepared with *garlic*?!

SOPHIE. (*Already off.*) It always is!

VAN. Then *that* explains why Dracula went for a stroll instead of eating! (*Exits, as we hear:*)

BORIS. (*Already off.*) He *also* had something more *attractive* to feed on!

NELLY. (*Who has finally moved* U. *near french doors.*) Don't *remind* me! (*But there is no reply as she carefully shuts and secures the double doors, then backs slowly* D. *almost to the table, on:*) There! That should help a little. At least—it *looks* too solid for anyone to pass through! I just wish they hadn't left me *alone*! (*And* DRACULA—*arms outstretched with his cloak, briefly, so that he seems momentarily a gigantic bat—rises up into view behind her [*Don't *see SPECIAL EFFECTS; he has been lying under the table (on a comfortable pad or mattress, it is hoped) since the Act Two curtain], completely blocking her from our view until he lowers his arms, which he does just before speaking.*)

DRACULA. They *didn't*!

NELLY. (*Whirls, reacts.*) Count Dracula! What do you want? (*She backs slightly toward* U.R., *he following ominously.*)

DRACULA. Sustenance. Food. A nice little snack to tide me over until Mina gets rid of that garlic!

NELLY. Uh . . . can I offer you a drink—?

DRACULA. I was *hoping* you'd say that . . .

NELLY. Wait. Stop. I didn't mean that the way it sounded!

DRACULA. Come, now, Nelly, cease this useless attempt at evasion. I cannot be escaped. Why try to fight it?

NELLY. I can think of several reasons: All puncture-marks.

DRACULA. Ah, then you *saw* Mina's little—shall we say—souvenirs?

NELLY. Shall we say "battle scars"?! . . . Say— (*Curiosity overcomes her fear, on:*) How come there were *three* of those little thingies on her neck?

DRACULA. Only two of them were made by me. Unfortunately, my castle is infested with rather large mosquitoes!

NELLY. (*Sympathetically.*) *That* can't be much fun. You ought to have somebody *exterminate* them!

DRACULA. Why do you think I hooked up with *Renfield*?! (*Starts moving toward her again.*) But we're wasting time. Come to me, Nelly. Come to me now.

NELLY. (*One short backstep.*) No. Go away. I don't like you. You're spooky!

DRACULA. Ah, the fragile little flower trembles with anticipation—!

NELLY. The fragile little flower is about to belt you in the snoot!

DRACULA. Nonsense! Gaze deep into my eyes, and see there the longing, the yearning, that must make you bend to my will!

NELLY. I don't want to! I won't! Keep away from me, you creep! (*MUSIC intros; it is that strange dance, again, but this time the female partner manages to keep backing away, this way and that, no matter how suavely the male approaches her, as:*)

DRACULA. (*Sings.*)
DON'T BE AFRAID!

NELLY. (*Sings right back at him.*)
NOW LISTEN—

DRACULA.
BELONG TO ME!

NELLY.
IT'S RATHER LATE—

DRACULA.

WE CAN'T EVADE—
  NELLY.
OH, PLEASE, SIR—
  DRACULA.
OUR DESTINY!
  NELLY.
I'D RATHER WAIT!
  DRACULA.
LOOK IN MY EYES!
  NELLY.
THEY'RE AWF'LY RED!
  DRACULA.
YOU CANNOT FLEE!
  NELLY.
BUT I CAN TRY!
  DRACULA.
YOU REALIZE—
  NELLY.
DON'T LOSE YOUR HEAD!
  DRACULA.
YOU'RE MEANT TO BE—
(*From here on,* NELLY *ceases to alternate lyrics with him, but
    simply sings babblingly onward, no matter how seductively
    he pursues her, thus:*)

DRACULA.	NELLY.
WITH ME	LET'S NOT BE
ETERNALLY!	HASTY! I
COME, SATISFY	HAVE OTHER FISH
MY ENSLAVING	TO FRY!
CRAVING!	YOU'RE NOT MY TYPE,
RELIEVE THE RAVING	FOR ONE THING,
HUNGER IN MY HEART!	AND BESIDES, I
IT'S TIME TO START!	FEEL LIKE
NOW YOU SHALL SURELY	RUNNING OFF TO
FIND	HIDE!
DARK DELIGHT!	FURTHERMORE, I'D LIKE
DON'T DECLINE!	TO STATE,
YOU ARE MINE	I NEVER EVEN *KISS* ON
TONIGHT!	THE FIRST DATE!
	PERHAPS IN TIME—I'LL
	TELL YOU WHEN—
	IF YOU THINK I'M

NELLY.
CONTENT
TO BE YOUR DRINKING
FOUNTAIN,
BETTER
THINK
AGAIN!

(*Weird final music trills in vain; she is still a good arm's length away from him.*)

DRACULA. (*Ceases pursuit.*)
AW, COME ON!

NELLY. (*Shrugs.*)
OH, WHAT THE HELL, WHY NOT!? (*She lurches happily into his arms, embraces him, leans her head back, and speaks directly into his face, extending the word, and making the "h"-sound as breathily aspirate as possible.*) Hiii!

DRACULA. (*Recoils with a cry, shoving her free of him.*) *Hey*! What the hell have you been *eating*?!

NELLY. Just a little pot roast . . .?! What's the matter? Too much garlic?

DRACULA. (*Now backing away from her pursuit.*) Don't you ever brush your teeth?!

NELLY. Listen, kiddo, *your* breath is *no* bed of roses! The last time I smelled anything like that, I was taking a tour of a slaughterhouse! (*They are now just* U. *of fireplace, his back almost to the wall.*)

DRACULA. Keep away from me!

NELLY. But you said you wanted me!

DRACULA. Not any more!

NELLY. (*Lunges for him.*) Aw, come on! (*And again there is a puff of smoke, and from it an enormous bat soars toward* U.C. *exit—except that doors are closed, and it crashes into the crack between the closed doors and slides stunned to the floor [see SPECIAL EFFECTS]; at this moment,* VAN, BUBU, SOPHIE, SAM *and* BORIS *rush in,* U.R., *see the fallen bat, and come to a horrified halt.*)

VAN. Look out! It's Count Dracula!

BUBU. He's not so *tall* as I remember.

NELLY. (*Hurrying up to join group, as they surround the fallen bat, completely blocking it from view.*) Be careful! He's only temporarily stunned, and it's still night time!

SOPHIE. (*As she and* SAM *take hold of handles of opposite doors.*) Quickly, let's put him outside!

SAM. Move back, all of you, you're blocking the doors!

VAN. Stop! Don't set him *free* again! Let's kill him while we have the chance!

BUBU. Right! Quick, stuff some garlic down his throat!

VAN. I used it all up protecting Mina!

BORIS. And wasn't *that* fun-and-a-half!

VAN. Look out! He's awakening! (ALL *scream—and both doors get flung wide—and* ALL *run backward down partway toward sofa, fanning out in fairly even stage-width distribution—as* DRACULA *stands up into our view as* OTHERS *scatter [see SPECIAL EFFECTS], his arms out-thrust bat-like in his cape, giving a roar of triumph.*)

SOPHIE. Oh, Sam! What'll we do *now*?!

SAM. Let's consult with an *expert*!

VAN. Don't look at *me*!

BUBU. But you're the *only* expert in the room!

VAN. And *I'm* all out of *garlic*!

SAM. Nelly! Hurry to the kitchen and get some more!

NELLY. We used it all up on the pot roast!

BUBU. Then go get *that*!

SOPHIE. Bubu, we can't swat a member of *royalty* with a *pot roast*!

BORIS. We could sprinkle him with the *gravy*—?!

DRACULA. (*Dropping his arms to his sides, taking a step forward.*) *Silence*! (ALL *freeze in fear, watching him.*) It's no use! You have lost! I am too powerful to resist!

VAN. You forget, Count Dracula, that the dawn will be coming up in a matter of minutes!

DRACULA. By then, I shall be safe in the hidden depths of my castle! And Mina shall be with me!

VAN. We'll find you! We'll destroy you!

DRACULA. Not if *I* destroy *you*—all of you—before I go!

BUBU. No! No! You wouldn't!

BORIS. That's all *you* know!

DRACULA. Enough! Your fate is sealed! You cannot move, any of you! Not so much as your little finger!

SOPHIE. Good grief! He's right!

NELLY. I feel like I'm set in cement!

BUBU. Oh, Van, Van, is there *nothing* you can do?

VAN. Without my garlic, I am powerless!

SAM. Then all of us are doomed!

DRACULA. Of course you are! (*MUSIC intros, and he sings, with rising fiendish glee.*)
YOU HAVEN'T GOT A CHANCE!
YOU CANNOT FIGHT THE GRAVE!
ONE FLICKER OF MY GLANCE
AND YOU'RE A HELPLESS SLAVE!
YOU CAN'T SAVE MINA NOW!
SHE'S MINE ETERNALLY!
WITH MY POWERS IMMORTAL,
THERE'S NO WAY TO THWART MY DECREE!
YOU ARE HELPLESS TO OUTRUN DISASTER!
NONE CAN MASTER ME!
                    (*Takes another step forward.*)
And now, all of you, prepare to die!

BORIS. (*Scuttles a few steps toward him.*) *All? All* of us? *Surely* you're not including *me*?

VAN. Boris! You can move!

BUBU. Oh, that's right, his powers only work on *normal* people!

SOPHIE. Save us, Boris!

SAM. You're the only one who can!

NELLY. Please? Pretty please? Nice nutso! Nice, *nice* nutso . . .?!

DRACULA. I am afraid all of you are wasting your breath! Even if he *is* free to move about, Boris is still the slave of my power, and must therefore do anything that his master chooses!

BORIS. (*As usual.*) *Master chooses*?! (OTHERS *will, of course, during upcoming song, be freed from* DRACULA's *spell, but they're still stuck in* BORIS's *mad-dance enthusiasm, as he sings.*)
A STATE THAT I THOUGHT WAS
SO VERY NICE!
IF YOU'LL TAKE MY ADVICE,
YOU'LL TURN YOUR FACES TO
THAT PLACE OF FEW REGRETS
CALLED MASS-A-CHU-SI-ETTS!
                    (*Same slow-to-fast development.*)
HYANNIS PORT IS FULL OF ODD FISH,
AND THE CAPE IS FULL OF CODFISH,
NEWPORT'S FULL OF SUBMARINES,
AND BOSTON'S FULL OF MORE THAN BEANS,
AND MASSACHUSETTS INSTITUTE
IS QUITE NEAR CAMBRIDGE, CHELSEA,

SOMMERVILLE, AND GOOD OLD NEWTON TO BOOT!
(*Same mad dance ensues, this time with* VAN, SAM *and* BORIS
doing square-dance-type "handaround" of BUBU, SOPHIE
and NELLY *from one to the other, in a ring around*
DRACULA, *who mostly whirls like a dervish; at dance's end,*
VAN *recovers equilibrium first, and:*)

VAN. Grab him! Grab him quickly, while he's still reeling
from the dance! He can't use his powers while he's dizzy! (ALL
move—slightly staggering from dizziness—toward DRACULA,
who staggers toward U.C..)

DRACULA. Back! All of you, back! You cannot kill one of the
undead!

BUBU. Well, we're sure gonna give it a try!

SAM. But *how*?! We have no weapons—!

SAM. Yes we have! We all had pot roast with *garlic* for dinner!

BORIS. We can pin him *down*—

NELLY. And *breathe* him to death!

DRACULA. (*On front edge of platform below* U.C., *now, suddenly draws himself up to his full height.*) Freeze! (ALL *do so.*)
I'm quite recovered, now, and you are all going to pay the dread
price for trifling with me! Prepare to die! (*A pink glow begins
from offstage* R. *of* U.C. *doorway.*)

VAN. No! *You* prepare! For look—there in the sky—!

SOPHIE/SAM. It's a bird—

BUBU/BORIS. It's a plane—

NELLY. It's— (ALL, *including* DRACULA, *jam fists against hips
and lean toward* VAN, *considerably dubuious, as they ask in in-
credulous unison:*)

ALL BUT VAN. —*Superman*?!

VAN. No! Even better! It is the blessed *dawn*!

DRACULA. Yipe! It *can't* be! It's *much* too early! (*Rushes up to
rail to look out right, on:*) I've never miscalculated *before* . . .?!
(*Looks, blows out his cheeks in a sigh of relief, drags the back of
one wrist across his brow, and steps back toward them, on:*)
Boy, *that's* a load off my mind! I *knew* it couldn't be the sunrise!

OTHERS. (*As pink glow redder and brighter.*) Then what the
hell *is* it?!

DRACULA. (*Happily relieved.*) Just the light from the flames
of my burning castle. (*Realizes abruptly, reacts with terror.*)
Burning castle!? My *coffin's* in there! Somebody *do* something!
Call the fire department—start a bucket brigade—pray for rain!
(*Springs up onto rail, bathed in fiery glow.*) This is terrible! This
is dreadful! This is totally intolerable!

SAM. (*Smilingly to* OTHERS, *briskly rubbing his palms together.*) Maybe from *his* point of view—!

BUBU. (*Points excitedly at what she sees.*) Hey, get a load of *that*! (*"That" is an even redder glow that suddenly lights* DRACULA *from behind—that is, from off left—as he faces fiery glow at right, wringing his hands; he senses it, turns, and shrieks.*)

DRACULA. *Sunrise*! Too long have I tarried! No coffin to which I can fly! No escape for me! Trapped between the ruination of my only refuge and the dawn of a new day! Doomed by the first sunrise I have ever seen—and also the last! Oh torment, oh pain, oh disaster—! (*Places back of wrist to forehead, tragically; then abruptly drops hand, looks left, and remarks casually:*) It *is* kind of *pretty*, though . . .! (*Then, back in doomed character, covers his face by wrapping himself in his cloak with both arms, and tumbles backward from our view with a LONG, DESPAIRING SCREAM, and BLACK SMOKE PUFFS UP from beyond rail.*)

VAN. (*As he and* OTHERS, *freed from the spell, rush to rail.*) The monster is destroyed! (ALL *lean over rail, backs to us, looking downward, over next six speeches.*)

BUBU. His cloak is tearing to tatters!

SAM. His shoes are turning to dust!

BUBU. His face is turning to steam!

NELLY. His clothing is turning to smoke!

SAM. He's turning into a flaming fireball!

VAN. And now there's nothing left but the morning mist and the rosy dawn! (ALL *turn in unison toward us, and:*)

ALL. (*Enthusiastically.*) Don't you wish *you'd* seen it?! (*Then* MINA, *still in night garb, but now bright-eyed, pink-cheeked, and healthy-looking as all-get-out, enters* U.R. *as* OTHERS *return via* U.C. *to platform.*)

MINA. What has happened? I feel as though I had awakened from some terrible dream!

NELLY. Oh, did *you* ever miss the *excitement*!

SAM. Let's not talk about it now! What *we* all need is a good stiff drink! (ALL *ad-lib sentiments of thirsty agreement, then they move gratefully down toward to table, during:*)

SOPHIE. It feels so peaceful with that monster gone.

BUBU. Yes, it does. The storm is past—

NELLY. The dawn is breaking—

SAM. The evil spell has been shattered—

MINA. And I washed off all the garlic! (ALL *are just above table, now, but nobody touches a glass or bottle, because—as you will see—there is no point in encumbering the cast with props for the final moments of the play that follow.*)

VAN. We are all most fortunate. Vampires do not perish without a struggle, and Count Dracula certainly struggled against his destruction with might and main!

BORIS. (*That wild light in his eyes again.*) Maine! (OTHERS *recoil in anticipatory horror, and freeze in those positions until* BORIS *suddenly slumps, and the light dies in his eyes as he remarks casually:*) Never *been* there! (OTHERS *snap gratefully out of their freeze, and* SAM *is just reaching for a decanter when* JONATHAN HARKER *enters via* U.L. *archway; he is tall, extremely curly-haired [this is a wig, of course], dressed in a light brown tweed business suit, and in every way possible looks extremely different from the man we recently saw plunge to his doom beyond the rail.*)

JONATHAN. Ah there! Good morning!

ALL. (*Turn, see him, gasp, then cry.*) Jonathan Harker!

MINA. You're alive!

JONATHAN. No thanks to Count Dracula, I assure you! He's had me prisoner in the dungeon of his castle for weeks, now. But tonight, I escaped from my chains, set fire to his coffin, tiptoed across the swamp, and here I am, safe and sound at last! (*Frowns.*) But I could tell you things that would curl your hair!

OTHERS. So we notice!

JONATHAN. But enough of this idle chatter! It is time to be reunited with my darling one, after lo these many lonely weeks! (JONATHAN *extends his arms, rushing into room;* MINA *extends her arms, rushing toward him; and* NELLY *extends her own arms, and simply waits, as* JONATHAN *rushes right past* MINA *to her;* MINA *belatedly stops her rush and turns, bewildered.*)

MINA. Jonathan! That woman you are embracing is our family *maid*, Nelly Norton!

NELLY. Of course it is! Who did you *think* he was coming back to?

MINA. But the day you left, you gave Nelly a note, and it said, "My dearest darling, when I return, you shall be my bride!"

JONATHAN. Yes, that's true, but the note was for *Nelly!*

MINA. Then why did she give it to *me* to read?!

NELLY. (*Shrugs.*) I was *bragging!* (*Snuggles up to* JONATHAN.) Oh, my darling, hold me!

SOPHIE. (*Same business with* SAM.) Oh, *my* darling, hold *me!*

BUBU. (*Quickly, as* MINA *looks tentatively toward* VAN, *rushes to him, embraces him, and declares:*) *This* one's taken, *too!*

MINA. I can see that, in the race for romance, I got a bit behind!

VAN. (*To* BUBU.) Vampires will stoop to anything!

BORIS. (*Shyly.*) *I* ain't got nobody to hug, Miss Mina . . .

MINA. But Boris—*you* are a certified *screwball!*

BORIS. Yeah, but in a family like *yours*, who'd ever *notice*?!

MINA. You've got a point there! (*She rushes to his arms, and then all four happy couples come romping* D. *as MUSIC intros, and:*)

ALL. (*Sing.*)

AT LAST THE MONSTER IS DESTROYED!

NELLY.

HE'S LIQUIDATED, NOW!

BUBU.

AND MY FIANCE'S UNEMPLOYED!

VAN.

BUT VINDICATED, NOW!

WOMEN.

THE MAN WHO FRIGHTENED US SO MUCH
AND SO OFTEN,
JUST LOST HIS COFFIN, AND TURNED TO A
TINY LITTLE CINDER!

ALL.

THAT GHASTLY APPETITE IS CURBED!

VAN. (*To* BUBU.)

NO NEED TO FLEE, MY DEAR!

MINA.

AND I CAN SLUMBER UNDISTURBED!

BORIS. (*Cozily, though she reacts with uneasiness.*)

EXCEPT BY ME, MY DEAR!

SAM.

HOW SWEET TO KNOW WE'LL GO ON
SERVING HUMANITY!

WOMEN.

FROM THE UNCANNY, WE'RE BACK TO INSANITY!

BUBU.

NO MORE STRIVING TO CHECK
HYPNOTIC MICKEYS!

MINA.

NO MORE MARKS ON MY NECK!
   Boris. (*Warmly, making her even more uneasy.*)
EXCEPT FOR HICKEYS!
   Sophie.
NOW COOLER PASSIONS WE'LL EXPRESS
IN SENTIMENTAL NEED!
   Jonathan.
AS WE EXCHANGE A SWEET CARESS—
   Boris. (*Making* Mina's *eyes bulge with shock.*)
OR SHARE A CENTIPEDE!
   All.
NO NEED TO FIGHT THE SPELL APPLIED BY
THAT FEARSOME FELLA!
NO NEED TO FEED HIS ELEMENTAL REGIMEN!
LET'S DROP THE WHOLE IDEA!
IT'S SUCH A PANACEA
TO LIVE WITH DIGNITY AGAIN! . . . *Olé*!
      (*And ALL COUPLES start doing the Charleston,
        as the dawn comes rosily up, and—.*)

THE CURTAIN FALLS

SPECIAL RECOMMENDATIONS

1) Re Dracula's entrance U.C. on Boris's "Heeeere's Dracky!":
   If your Dracula is athletically equal to it, the entrance would
   be much more effective if he *springs* into view from down
   behind the balustrade, arms wide in cape for "bat"-effect,
   and lands *atop* the rail, before jumping down to balcony level
   and entering the room.

2) Some assists to the cast re characterization: The show is flexi-
   ble enough that variations in characters are permissible, but
   the *ideal* "type" of performance from each would be—

Sam:	Stuffy and obtuse
Sophie:	Fluttery and vague
Nelly:	Nervy but nervous
Mina:	Warmly romantic (except when in Dracula's thrall)
Bubu:	No-nonsense and brusque
Van:	Priggish but staunch
Boris:	Sneaky when not frenzied, now-and-then dopily shy
Dracula:	Suave and menacing, except for indicated breaks from character, such as during impatience with Boris or just before his final plunge
Jonathan:	Very stiff-upper-lip British

SPECIAL EFFECTS

1) THE BAT: You'll note that the false fireplace and desk both
   have a "shelf" inside, formed respectively by the log-chamber
   and the kneehole; the bat, hooked to a long wire running to a
   point upstage of and *above* the open U.C. doorway (so that it
   won't drag along the floor) is simply "flown" kite-fashion
   from this perch the moment Dracula has safely popped from
   view.

2) VANISHMENTS: All Dracula need do is stoop, roll into a
   knees-against-chest ball, roll on his back into either the gap at
   upstage side of fireplace or desk, then roll *sideways* to area
   behind the scenes, thus allowing clearance for the bat-launch.

3) MATERIALIZATION: For the startling effect of Dracula
   rising up from behind the chaise (and he should briefly do
   that bat-look bit with arms in cape as he rises), simply have
   him crouch waiting inside fireplace-escape until women

gather by fireplace to chat silently; the purpose of their blocking here is to make a "wall" spanning the gap between fireplace and chaise behind which "wall" Dracula can scuttle to a position behind chaise, to rise up seemingly impossibly once Mina is left there alone. As for his final materialization, once he has done the roll-escape from Nelly, he simply goes upstage of the closed french doors, crouches until Sophie and Sam have partly opened the doors (allowing the bat to be pulled through the gap by Dracula and slid aside for his abrupt standup into startling view), then simply springs to his feet from behind the "wall" of people (who are *by* the closed doors so that his crouched form and the departing bat cannot be seen when the doors are opened).

4) THE MIRROR: In previous editions of this script, an actual "trick mirror" was described that would reflect everybody *but* Dracula, in keeping with the vampire tradition. But then, on May 6th, 1968, I attended a production of the show at the Westminster (CA) Community Theatre, and their innovation had me *convulsed* with laughter, and from now on I'd like it done *their* way: As each *non*-vampire cast-member looked into the "mirror" (which was actually a *cutout* in the wall, with painted frame and a silver-paint-sprayed interior about six inches deep from the opening as "mirror-backdrop"), a wooden stick (about the shape/size of a yardstick) popped up into view with a life-size *photograph* (trimmed to the head-outlines) of that cast-member at the top; it would remain there while they primped, etc., then pop down again when they left. Then, when *Dracula* stepped to the mirror — a *bare stick* popped up into view. (The audience *shrieked* with laughter, and so did I.) Later, when *Mina* ("halfway to Vampireville") looked into the mirror, the stick with her photo popped up — and then flipped abruptly back-to-front, which is when she chided Nellie for not cleaning the mirror properly. I promise you, if you utilize *this* method in your production, the laughter/applause will be deafening.

5) THE FLOWERS: They are simply artificial flowers with limp rubber stems, bound into an upright position by a loop of thread that passes through a minuscule hole in the wall over the pier table and is anchored to a pole or joist or somesuch thing. When the time comes for their collapse, the thread is simply cut backstage, and down they go. [Note that the flowers that droop in Act Two obviously *cannot* be the ones Nelly brings on to replace the droopy ones in Act One, since the thread must be passed through the hole, fastened, etc., before the effect will work. So you will

need a vase of stiff-stemmed *duplicates* of the Act Two flowers for Nelly to bring on during Act One. The new droop-mechanism—like the second-act bat-mechanism—is set up between the acts.]

SUPPLEMENT TO

DRACULA:

The Musical?

Specially written by Rick Abbot for theatre groups who wish to do "DRACULA: The *Musical?*" with casts in excess of eight people.

TABLE OF CONTENTS

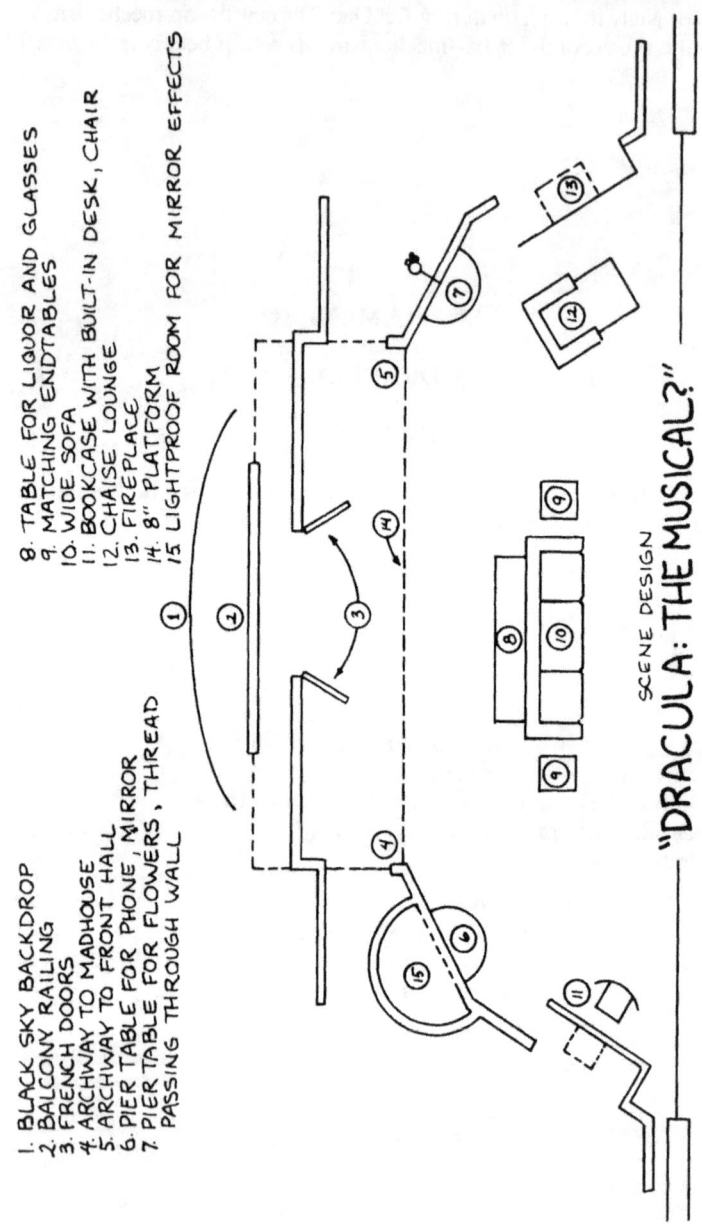

1. BLACK SKY BACKDROP
2. BALCONY RAILING
3. FRENCH DOORS
4. ARCHWAY TO MADHOUSE
5. ARCHWAY TO FRONT HALL
6. PIER TABLE FOR PHONE, MIRROR
7. PIER TABLE FOR FLOWERS, THREAD
   PASSING THROUGH WALL

8. TABLE FOR LIQUOR AND GLASSES
9. MATCHING ENDTABLES
10. WIDE SOFA
11. BOOKCASE WITH BUILT-IN DESK, CHAIR
12. CHAISE LOUNGE
13. FIREPLACE
14. 8" PLATFORM
15. LIGHTPROOF ROOM FOR MIRROR EFFECTS

SCENE DESIGN

"DRACULA: THE MUSICAL?"

58

Large-Cast Version of "DRACULA: The *Musical?*"

OPENING OF SHOW

Curtain-rise finds stage filled with LUNATICS, each costumed according to his or her delusion (this can be a wide variety of costumes, but must *include those persons named in the upcoming song); they are in small groups here and there, chatting. NELLY enters* U.L., *sees them all, reacts with tolerant annoyance, and:*

NELLY. Do you know what *time* it is?!

CAESAR. Aw, Nelly, have a heart!

NELLY. (*kindly but firmly*) Your supper break is one hour! You've been out of your cells for nearly two!

NAPOLEON. Aw, where's the harm?! Even certified *lunatics* gotta have *some* kind of recreation!

NELLY. An hour after supper is plenty! Now, come on, all of you, back to your cells! Doctor Seward will be simply *furious* if he finds you here!

QUEEN OF BABYLON. Don't be such a stick-in-the-mud, Nelly! Why not join the fun?

OTHERS. Yeah!

(*MUSIC INTROS, and all [except NELLY] do the following number, their actions—where appropriate—matching the actions described in the lyric.*)

ALL. (*sing*)
WE'RE HAVIN' A PARTY! WE'RE HAVIN' A BLAST!
THE MUSIC IS HEARTY! THE DANCIN' IS FAST!
MEN.
IN MERRY OLD ENGLAND, YOU WILL FIND FEW
 BALLS . . .
WOMEN.
. . . WHERE ALL OF THE GUESTS ARE CERTIFIED
 SCREWBALLS!
ALL.
FOR ANYONE LAZY, A DANCE IS HARD WORK!
YOU GOTTA BE CRAZY TO GO SO BERSERK!
IT'S BREAKIN' THE RULES A BIT, BUT
WE TAKE US A CHANCE,
AND HAVE US A DEEP-DEPRAVITY DANCE!

MEN.
CAESAR DANCES SLOWLY IN
HIS TOGA CLEAN AND BRIGHT!
WOMEN.
THEN THERE COMES NAPOLEON
TO JOSEPHINE'S DELIGHT!
ALL.
GOLIATH'S WITH THAT VERY PERT
YOUNG QUEEN OF BABYLON,
AND WHERE ELSE COULD DuBARRY FLIRT
WITH SCARY GENGHIS [pr. "JENG-iss"] KHAN?
SO . . .
WE'RE HAVIN' A PARTY WHERE EV'RYONE STRUTS!
THE DANCIN' IS ARTY! THE SINGERS ARE NUTS!
MEN.
WHEN LADY GODIVA'S PRANCIN' WITH NERO . . .
WOMEN.
. . . WHO CARES IF OUR GROUP MENTALITY'S ZERO?
ALL.
YOU REALLY CAN'T BLAME US FOR LACKING A
    BRAIN:
WE'D RATHER BE FAMOUS THAN STODGY AND SANE!
IT'S REALLY NO MYST'RY WHY WE
REMAIN AS WE ARE . . .
PSYCHOSIS MAKES YOUR LIFE MERRY!
WHO WANTS TO BE ORDINARY?
IT'S REALLY A BALL TO BE BIZARRE!
(*All dance wildly while sustaining final note, but stop on final accompaniment-chord.*)

NELLY. That was lovely! Now, back to your cells before I set the *dogs* on you!

(*LUNATICS mumble, but exit* U.R.; *NELLY remains* U.C. *arms folded, tapping her foot and watching them go; when the last has gone, she gives a satisfied nod, then starts toward* U.L., *but stops when phone rings, and:* pick up with NEL-LY's *dialogue top of page 6 in original script.*)

(*FIRST INSERT: At top of page 32 in original script, as soon as BUBU says,* "Van, darling, you *are asking us to swallow quite a tall story—!",* the following occurs: MALE VIL-*

LAGER — dressed in lederhausen, feathered Tyrolean hat, etc. — rushes in via U.L., *stops.*)

M.V. Are we in *time?!*

NELLY. In time for *what?*

SAM. Who *are* you, anyhow?

M.V. (*as other VILLAGERS — MEN dressed as he is, and WOMEN in peasant dresses, babushkas, etc. — enter* U.L.:) We are angry villagers, seeking out the crypt of Count Dracula, so we may destroy him!

SOPHIE. But where are your *torches?*

FEMALE VILLAGER. In the rack in the downstairs hall.

M.V. Didn't want to smoke up the parlor.

SAM. But, confound it, this is *England!* We don't *have* angry villagers!

F.V. Oh, but *we're* not *from* England!

VAN. Then — where *did* you come from?!

M.V. Where *else?!*

(*MUSIC INTROS and:*)

VILLAGERS. (*sing*)
ALL THE WAY FROM TRANSYLVANIA
IN A CATTLEBOAT'S HOLD
FILLED WITH GRIT AND GRUESOME GRAINY
ACCUMULATIONS OF MOLD,
ALL CRAMMED ON ONE TINY BENCH,
WE SAT IN THE STINK AND STENCH
DESPITE THE DISGUSTING MISCELLANEA,
AND DIDN'T NEED TO BE CONSOLED!
FOR . . .
(*During following refrain, the parenthetical lyrics are a sort of delayed-echo done by male voices.*)
WHEN THERE'S A CREA- (WHEN THERE'S A CREA-)
TURE TO DESTROY, (TURE TO DESTROY,)
OUR LITTLE HEARTS ARE FAIRLY
BOUNCING OUT WITH JOY! (JOY! JOY! JOY!)
WE NEVER MIND THE GRIND OF TRAVELING,
IF WE CAN DO THE THING
WE ALL ADORE!
WE TAKE OUR TOR- (WE TAKE OUR TOR-)
CHES IN OUR HAND, (CHES IN OUR HAND,)

AND TRAVEL ANYWHERE
ON SEA OR AIR OR LAND!
IT DOESN'T MATTER WHERE IT'S AT,
WE GO ON GALLOPING THROUGH THE GORE
FROM SINGAPORE . . .

MALES.

OR SOUTH LAHORE . . .

FEMALES.

TO BALTIMORE . . .

MALES.

OR LABRADOR . . .

ALL VILLAGERS.

'CAUSE THAT'S WHAT VILLAGERS ARE FOR!
(*MUSIC turns wistful, for:*)

MALES.

THERE ARE FIELDS TO PLOW . . .

FEMALES.

THERE ARE HORSES TO SHOE . . .

MALES.

THERE ARE SHEEP TO SHEAR . . .

FEMALES.

THERE IS BEER TO BREW . . .

ALL VILLAGERS.

THERE ARE COWS TO MILK. THERE ARE MAIDENS TO
   WOO.
BUT WHEN CREATURES CREEP ABOUT, THERE IS
   JUST ONE THING TO DO . . .
(*MUSIC returns to upbeat tempo for:*)
WE TAKE OUR TOR- (WE TAKE OUR TOR-)
CHES FROM THE RACK, (CHES FROM THE RACK,)
AND SING AND SHOUT AS WE SET OUT
UPON HIS TRACK! (TRACK! TRACK! TRACK!)
IF HE'S IN GERMANY OR BURMA,
OR THE JUNGLES OF ECUADOR,
WE ALL SET OFF TO FIND HIS COFFIN
WITH A WHOOP AND A MIGHTY ROAR!
THROUGH STORM AND FLOOD AND MUCK AND MUD
AND MURK AND SHUDDERY TOMBS GALORE!
'CAUSE THAT'S WHAT VILLAGERS ARE FOR!
(THAT'S WHAT WE'RE FOR! THAT'S WHAT WE'RE
   FOR!
THAT'S WHAT WE'RE FOR!) OH. . . . YEAH!

VAN. (*to SAM*) There! You *see?* This *proves* that vampires exist!

SAM. What? The opinion of a bunch of illegal aliens? Don't be ridiculous, Van Helsing!

VAN. (*gives it up*) There's no time to argue! (*clutches BORIS*) Renfield! Can *you* lead me and these villagers to the monster's lair?

BORIS. What?! Approach a vampire's castle by crossing a swamp on foot in the middle of the night with a thunderstorm coming up? Only a *crazy* man would try it!

VAN. You *are* a crazy man!

BORIS. Then what are we *waiting* for?!

(*BORIS, VAN and VILLAGERS dash out* U.L. *Pick up with SAM's "Of all things!" on page 32, and continue in original script.*)

(*SECOND INSERT: Bottom of page 35 in original script, after BORIS says, "No point in catching cold. . . !":*)

BUBU. But what about all those villagers you left with?

BORIS. (*shrugs*) I guess they're still searching—if the quicksand didn't get 'em!

(*Pick up with VAN's "Good grief! What are you ladies wearing?!" and continue in original script.*)

(*THIRD INSERT: Near bottom of page 47 in original script. When DRACULA turns to smoke, then into bat, and flies toward* U.C. *doors, the doors will open magically just before he gets there, and bat will fly out into night; then VAN, BUBU, SOPHIE, SAM and BORIS rush in* U.R., *stop, and:*)

VAN. We heard unearthly screaming!

NELLY. (*annoyed*) That was me, *singing!*

BORIS. What is there to *sing* about?

NELLY. Count Dracula was just here. But he turned into a bat and got away.

SAM. Aha! Then it *wasn't* a coincidence!

NELLY. *What* wasn't?

SOPHIE. *Mina* just did the very same thing!

NELLY. Turned into a *bat* and flew off into the *night?!*

BUBU. Yes! Right toward Dracula's castle!

NELLY. That's horrible! We've got to *save* her!

VAN. Right! Nighttime or not — we've got to find our way *into* that castle and wipe that monster *out,* once and for all! Are you with me?

OTHERS. *Yeaaah!*

(*ALL rush toward* U.L., *and we have a BLACKOUT. [NOTE: During this blackout, curtains will close so that the crypt-set can be erected onstage; this will consist of three walls, with windows — stained glass, if possible — at upper part of each wall-segment; sofa and table should be moved up onto platform behind back flat of crypt, and a white coffin bearing the Dracula crest should be on a white-draped catafalque just about two feet downstage of crypt's* U.C. *wall; it will have no lid, or — if a lid is used — it must be the sort that can be lifted clear of the coffin and set aside, for easier access to Dracula when he's in it.] As soon as BLACKOUT starts, MUSIC INTROS, and those VILLAGERS — grouped via voice-ranges — will enter up various aisles, in the order indicated, and end up on stage apron before closed curtain; spotlights can come up on curtain as soon as singing begins.*)

BARITONES. (*sing*)

OH, HOW OUR FIRM RESOLVE'S STARTING TO
    SOFTEN,
CREEPING ALONG IN THE DARK OF THE MOON,
QUIETLY LOOKING FOR DRACULA'S COFFIN,
HOPING HE DOESN'T WAKE UP TOO SOON!

CONTRALTOS.

NIGHT AIR'S SO UNHEALTHY
OVER THIS MARSHY GROUND!
CAREFUL, NOW! STAY STEALTHY!
HUSH, OH HUSH, NOT A SOUND!

(*BARITONES and CONTRALTOS will now repeat their verses in unison/counterpoint; then:*)

TENORS. (*moving up aisle toward apron*)

FLIT ALONG ON FOOTSTEPS FACILE!

CAREFULLY, IT'S NOT QUITE DAWN!
OH, PENETRATE THE VAMPIRE'S CASTLE
LIKE A MOUSE WITH SNEAKERS ON!

(*BARITONES, CONTRALTOS and TENORS will now repeat
their verses in unison/counterpoint; then:*)

SOPRANOS. (*moving up aisle toward apron*)
HUSH, NOW! LET'S GO! OH, MY-OH-ME!
SOFTLY TIPTOE! CREEP, CREEP QUIETLY!

(*ALL VILLAGERS now repeat respective lyrics in unison/
counterpoint, and ALL are intermingled on stage-apron by
the time they finish in unison:*)

ALL VILLAGERS.
PRAY HE'S NOT BEHIND YOU!
VAMPIRES LIKE TO KILL!
BE STILL!

(*On final chord of song, VILLAGERS all look about them,
fearfully, and lights fade quickly to black; after about five
seconds [during which curtains open in darkness and PRIN-
CIPALS and VILLAGERS get into positions in crypt] lights
come up full in crypt; MINA is standing behind coffin,
trancelike and still; DRACULA is standing before coffin,
facing DS., VILLAGERS are lined along left and right walls
of crypt, with VAN, BUBU and SOPHIE with left group,
and SAM, NELLY and BORIS with right group; ALL are
facing toward DRACULA, and the instant lights come up,
ALL react, cringe back slightly, and:*)

ALL. (*in unison*)
OH HELL! WE'VE *FOUND* HIM!

(*Pick up on page 48 of original script, with SOPHIE's "Oh,
Sam! What'll we do now?! and continue in original script to
next insert.*)

(*FOURTH INSERT: Center of page 50 in original script.
[NOTE: During mad gypsy dance preceding this insert,
VILLAGERS will dance and sing along with PRIN-*

CIPALS.] As soon as DRACULA completes his speech with ". . . Prepare to die!": a pink glow begins out side the windows, and will reach full brightness [very bright, as on a sunny morning] by end of next song number.)

VAN. No! *You* prepare! Too long have you tarried, evil count! There comes the blessed dawn!

DRACULA. (*staggered*) Boris! This is all *your* fault! You and your contagious enthusiasm! I feel faint . . . I've got to lie down . . . (*will clamber into his coffin during:*) Uh . . . now look, everybody . . . while I'm lying in here, catatonic and helpless . . . uh . . . *be kind—?!* (*sags from sight, flat on his back in coffin*)

VAN. Quickly! Who's got a mallet?

M.V. (*producing one*) Here!

VAN. And who's got a stake?

BUBU. I think I have one in my handbag! (*Reaches into handbag—no bigger than a coin purse—and slowly pulls out two-foot wooden pointed stake. [NOTE: This visual gag is simple: The stake is actually hidden inside her full skirt, with an opening near her waist; the handbag has an opening in the back; when she reaches into the bag—held against her waist in the front—she simply pulls the stake out through the hole in the bag until the entire thing is in view.*)

VAN. My! You're just *full* of surprises, Bubu! (*He moves up behind coffin, places point of stake on unseen DRACULA's chest [actually between player's DS. arm and ribcage], and raises mallet.*)

BUBU. (*rushes up beside him*) Here, let me help you, darling! (*Takes hold of stake, which he then releases.*) I'll hold . . . you hammer!

VAN. Why, darling! I thought my work disgusted you!

BUBU. It does. But a wife should support her husband in his career! After all—marriage should be founded on *trust!*

VAN. Naturally—but—what has holding the stake got to do with trust?

BUBU. I'm trusting you not to mash my thumb with that mallet!

NELLY. (*sighs wistfully*) Isn't that just the most romantic thing you ever heard?!

OTHERS except VAN and BUBU. It surely is!

(*VAN raises mallet, MUSIC INTROS [NOTE: During song, the stressed syllables indicate the moments when VAN will pound the mallet on the stake. He must not pound except on these syllables, since the fun of this ghastly song is in its persistently jolly rhythmics], and:*)

BUBU.
TAKE THE MALLET IN YOUR HAND,
FOR, MY DEAR, I UNDERSTAND
WHEN THE STAKE I START TO SHOVE . . .
IT'S THE *TIPPY-TIPPY-TAP OF LOVE!*
  DRACULA. (*groaned*) Oh, woe!

(*NOTE: He will raise his head into view on each of his lines in song, then immediately drop his head back out of our view again — a sort of cuckoo-clock comic effect.*)

VAN.
THERE IS SOMETHING SO BENIGN
WITH YOUR CHEEK SO CLOSE TO MINE
AS THE GORE GETS ON YOUR GLOVE . . .
TO THE *TIPPY-TIPPY-TAP OF LOVE!*
  DRACULA. (*groaned*) Oh, no!

(*As song continues, all but BUBU and VAN start romantic swaying left and right to musical beat, arms about each others' waists, smiling cheerily no matter how grisly matters get; and from the time BORIS starts singing, matters do get grisly: From unseen interstices in coffin-front, red liquid begins to run down onto white drape on catafalque. [NOTE: Either use disappearing ink for this, or have high-gloss white enamel on coffin and white vinyl for the drape, so cleanups between shows will be easy]; this flow increases in speed and volume to song's end.*)

BORIS.
AS THE *MAG-IC* MOMENT *STARTS,*
AND YOUR *PREY* GETS DE-*PRESSED* . . .
  NELLY.
MATCH THE *POUND-ING* OF YOUR *HEARTS*
TO THE *POUND-ING* ON HIS *CHEST!*

DRACULA. (*groaned*) Ah, Me!

ALL. (*singing and swaying like crazy*)
SEE HIM FLUTTER LIKE A DOVE
AS THE NEW DAY DAWNS ABOVE,
AND THE SCREAM YOU'RE DREAMING OF . . .

DRACULA. (*Sings, then drops his head back from our view.*)
OH, GEE!

ALL.
. . . FROM THE *VAM*-PIRE IN A *TRAP*
RISES *LIKE* A THUNDER-*CLAP*
TO THE *TIP*-PY-*TIP*-PY-*TAP* . . .
OF . . .
LOVE!

(*And on final accompaniment-chord, VAN strikes final blow,
and drops mallet from view behind coffin, and triumphantly
dusts off his hands.*)

MINA. (*sways, blinks, looks about*) What has happened? I
feel as though I had awakened from some terrible dream!

NELLY. Oh, did *you* ever miss the excitement!

VAN. We are all most fortunate. Vampires do not perish
without a struggle, and Count Dracula certainly struggled
against his destruction with might and main!

BORIS. (*that wild light in his eyes again*) Maine! (*OTHERS
recoil in anticipatory horror — and then he suddenly slumps,
pouts, shrugs, and finishes:*) Never *been* there!

MINA. Oh, dear! I just realized — with Dracula gone, how are
we ever to learn what has become of Jonathan Harker?!

M.V. No need to worry, Mina! For, you see, *I* am Jonathan
Harker! (*whips off Tyrolean hat to reveal head of curly hair*)
Dracula held me prisoner in his dungeon in Transylvania, but I
managed to escape, disguised myself as a peasant villager, and
joined the first group I could find heading out to seek the
Count!

BUBU. It must have been *awful* for you!

JONATHAN. It certainly was! I could tell you things that would
curl your hair!

(*Pick up with preceding line on page 52 of original script, and
continue to end of show, VILLAGERS singing in the
"ALL" parts of show's final musical number and dancing at*

final curtain. NOTE: Since DRACULA's demise in the expanded-cast version of the show differs from his demise in the 8-player version, the single line describing that demise in the show's finale must be altered, thus: Where the original script/score has:)

WOMEN.
THE MAN WHO FRIGHTENED US SO MUCH
AND SO OFTEN,
JUST LOST HIS COFFIN, AND TURNED TO A
TINY LITTLE CINDER!
(*substitute the new line:*)
THE MAN WHO HAD OUR LITTLE MINDS
IN A MUDDLE,
TURNED TO A PUDDLE, AND MESSED UP HIS
PRETTY LITTLE COFFIN!

[TWO NOTES ON PREMIERE OF LARGE-CAST VERSION (at Bell High School in Bell, California):

1) When BORIS shouts "Master chooses!" and all recoil, a disheartened-but-resigned DRACULA reaches into his coffin, takes out a tambourine, and hands it to BORIS, who says a polite "Thank you," with a slight bow, and *then* launches into his song, augmenting the piano-accompaniment with use of the tambourine.

2) Instead of having "blood" oozing down coffinside during song, DRACULA had a turkey-baster of "blood" hidden in the coffin, and at the *final* ". . . LOVE!" at end of song, squirted a huge *sploop* of "blood" vertically from the coffin to climax the song.

Both these innovations provoked *huge* laughs, and may be done by your group with my blessings.

Rick Abbot]

MUSIC USE NOTE

Licensees are solely responsible for obtaining formal written permission from copyright owners to use copyrighted music in the performance of this play and are strongly cautioned to do so. If no such permission is obtained by the licensee, then the licensee must use only original music that the licensee owns and controls. Licensees are solely responsible and liable for all music clearances and shall indemnify the copyright owners of the play(s) and their licensing agent, Samuel French, against any costs, expenses, losses and liabilities arising from the use of music by licensees. Please contact the appropriate music licensing authority in your territory for the rights to any incidental music.

IMPORTANT BILLING AND CREDIT REQUIREMENTS

If you have obtained performance rights to this title, please refer to your licensing agreement for important billing and credit requirements.

www.ingramcontent.com/pod-product-compliance
Lightning Source LLC
Chambersburg PA
CBHW070358120726
47909CB00008B/2901